D0389652

The Last Word

The Last Word

SAMANTHA HASTINGS

A Swoon Reads Book
An imprint of Feiwel and Friends and Macmillan Publishing Group, LLC
120 Broadway, New York, NY 10271

Our books may be purchased in bulk for promotional, educational, or business use.
Please contact your local bookseller or the Macmillan Corporate and Premium Sales Department
at (800) 221-7945 ext. 5442 or by email at MacmillanSpecialMarkets@macmillan.com.

Library of Congress Cataloging-in-Publication Data is available.
ISBN 978-1-250-30188-8 (hardcover) / ISBN 978-1-250-30187-1 (ebook)

Book design by Katie Klimowicz

First edition, 2019
1 3 5 7 9 10 8 6 4 2
swoonreads.com

For Jon

Women are supposed to be very calm generally: but women feel just as men feel; they need exercise for their faculties, and a field for their efforts as much as their brothers do; they suffer from too rigid a restraint, too absolute a stagnation, precisely as men would suffer; and it is narrow-minded in their more privileged fellow-creatures to say they ought to confine themselves to making puddings and knitting stockings, to playing on the piano and embroidering bags. It is thoughtless to condemn them, or laugh at them, if they seek to do more or learn more than custom has pronounced necessary for their sex.

—CHARLOTTE BRONTË, *JANE EYRE*

One

SHE WAS FINALLY GOING TO escape protocol prison.

Or, in other words, Miss Lucinda Leavitt was graduating from Miss Holley's Finishing School for Young Ladies, where she'd spent four aggravating years reluctantly obtaining polish and female accomplishments. She looked down at her pink dress—it had more layers than a wedding cake. She hoped her father would find it pretty and see that she was all grown up now. That she was able to make decisions for herself.

Miss Holley, the plump proprietor, came into the sitting room with another woman, who was extremely thin with a long face framed by mousy-brown braids.

"Miss Holley, by chance has my father arrived yet?" Lucinda asked.

Miss Holley sniffed. "Miss Leavitt, do not be presumptuous. Your father is a very important businessman, and he has better things to do with his time than accompany you home from school."

"Yes, ma'am, but I am to leave today. Will I be allowed to travel on the train to London alone?" Lucinda asked, unable to keep the excitement from her voice.

"Do not be fanciful, Miss Leavitt," Miss Holley said, shaking her head. "Young ladies of quality must be chaperoned at all times for their safety and for their reputation. 'For a lady's reputation is—' "

" 'As fragile as a flower,' " Lucinda finished without enthusiasm.

"I am glad you learned something at my school, Miss Leavitt," Miss Holley said. "Although not as much as I would have liked. But perhaps Mrs. Patton will be able to succeed where I have failed."

"Mrs. Patton?"

Miss Holley touched her massive bosom and said, "Dear me, I should have introduced you at the first, Lavinia. Miss Leavitt, allow me to introduce your new lady's companion, Mrs. Lavinia Patton. She is an old friend of mine."

"Companion? I don't need a companion," Lucinda said, rising.

"Manners, Miss Leavitt, manners," Miss Holley chided. "Your father has already hired Mrs. Patton upon my recommendation. She will introduce you to the best of society and help you become an elegant lady."

Lucinda curtsied to the long-faced woman. “I am pleased to make your acquaintance, Mrs. Patton. How long should I expect the pleasure of your company?”

Mrs. Patton bowed her head slightly. “Until you are married, dear girl. Which I should not think will be too long, given your face and fortune.”

“You forget her low birth . . . and that she is obstinate and headstrong, with a mind of her own,” Miss Holley said. “Still, if anyone can help Miss Leavitt to an advantageous match, it is you, Lavinia.”

But I don’t want to get married, Lucinda thought fiercely. *I want to work in my father’s countinghouse.*

Two weeks later, Lucinda bit her thumbnail in frustrated boredom.

Being an elegant lady is exceedingly dull work, she thought as she sat on the edge of her chair next to the window, waiting for the post to arrive. She had nothing else to do. It was too early in the day to make calls and too late in the day to lie in bed.

So she counted the carriages that passed the street in front of her house—thirty-two. She counted the people who walked by—forty-seven (twenty-three women and twenty-four men). She was about to count the bricks on the house across the street when the postman arrived. She jumped from her chair and ran to the door before the butler, Mr. Ruffles, could answer it. She flung open the door and startled the postman, who was opening the letter box.

"I'll take those," she said, reaching out her hand.

The postman touched his navy cap and bowed to her before handing her several letters and a small package.

"Thank you!" Lucinda said and shut the door. She turned to see Mr. Ruffles standing behind her. He bowed to her. He was shorter than Lucinda and had a square-shaped face and a mouth that never smiled.

"Here's the post, Ruffles," she said, handing him the stack of letters. They were all for her father anyway. She kept the small parcel clutched tightly in her white-knuckled hands, knowing exactly what it was. Lucinda skipped to the sitting room, where ladies sat . . . a lot. Her companion, Mrs. Patton, was already sleeping in a chair, snoring with her mouth open.

Lucinda quietly closed the door. She untied the twine and unwrapped the brown paper to reveal *Wheathill's Magazine*, the May 1861 edition. Lucinda squealed silently and hopped up and down on the balls of her feet.

It was finally here!

She sat down on the sofa, flipped open the cover, and found the table of contents. The newest installment of *She Knew She Was Right* by Mrs. Smith began on page thirty-six. Lucinda turned the pages quickly until she reached the correct page. There was an illustration—a young lady dressed in a ball gown with a gentleman on each side. Both gentlemen held one arm outstretched toward her. The caption underneath read: *Whom will she choose?* The same question had been plaguing Lucinda since she read the April edition of the magazine. Now, a month later, her curiosity was at last to be satiated. After two years of reading the book published in serial form, she was finally going to read the ending.

Lucinda held her breath and began to read:

> *"My feelings are like a tangled web, Miss Emerson," Lord Dunstan said as he clasped her delicate hand between his two large ones. "And only you can unravel them."*
>
> *Eurydice's heart fluttered and her face flushed with color. Lord Dunstan was so very tall, dark, and handsome, with only a slight white scar underneath his left ear to disfigure his otherwise natural beauty.*
>
> *"Lord Dunstan, I do believe you are flirting with me."*
>
> *"I am not flirting, my dear Miss Emerson," he said. "I am completely in earnest. You alone hold all of my affections. All of my dreams and wishes for my future are tangled up around you."*
>
> *Could this be a declaration? Eurydice could hardly breathe. Her heart beat wildly. She looked down at her feet, for she was too embarrassed to look him in the eye.*
>
> *"Miss Emerson, before I can beg you to be mine for all time, I must tell you the truth of my past."*
>
> *Eurydice was surprised enough by these words to*

look up into his dark, stormy eyes and hold her breath in terrible expectation.

"Lord Dunstan," Mr. Thisbe called from the door of the house. "Lord Dunstan, Mr. Emerson wishes to have speech with you."

"We will have to finish our conversation later, my dear Miss Emerson. I leave you most reluctantly," Lord Dunstan said, and kissed the top of Eurydice's hand before releasing it.

Eurydice could only nod, so great was her embarrassment. Lord Dunstan walked into the house, and Mr. Thisbe came out to the garden where Eurydice was picking flowers. He was not as tall nor as handsome as Lord Dunstan, but his blue eyes were open and kind. He had an air of virtue and humility. To Eurydice's shock, he knelt before her on the grass and took the same hand that Lord Dunstan had recently held and kissed.

"Miss Emerson," Mr. Thisbe said, "I believe that the Lord above ordained us for one another. Will you do me the great honor of becoming my wife?"

Lucinda's heart raced as if she'd run up a hill. Which suitor would Eurydice choose? But the next page was blank. Lucinda frowned, wondering if there had been some sort of misprint. When she continued on, the next page had a note from the editor:

Here the story is broken off, and it can never be finished. What promised to be the crowning work of a life is a memorial of death. The Editor regrets to inform the Reader that Mrs. Smith has died. But if the work is not quite complete, little remains to be added to it, and that little has been distinctly reflected into our minds. Which suitor would Eurydice Emerson have chosen? The handsome and mysterious Lord Dunstan, or the kind and generous Mr. Thisbe? Now we will never know.

Thomas Gibbs, Editor, 1861

"But I must know!" Lucinda said aloud.

She sat up in disbelief and quickly read the editor's note again. She bit the end of her thumbnail and blinked away tears that had formed in her eyes. Her favorite author could not have died. It was impossible. *Unthinkable.* Mrs. Smith's novels were Lucinda's only escape from the endless monotony of her existence.

Mrs. Patton awoke from her dozing. She blinked several times and brought her lace handkerchief to her mouth, sighing long and loud.

"Really, Lucinda," she chided in a singsong voice. "That is hardly a ladylike tone to be using."

"She's dead," Lucinda said numbly, and slumped back on the sofa, tears falling freely from her eyes. She wiped them away with the back of her hand.

"Who is dead?" Mrs. Patton asked, sitting up straight.

"The author of *She Knew She Was Right* is dead," Lucinda said with a sniffle. "And now the story will remain unfinished."

Mrs. Patton gave another long sigh and leaned back in her seat. "You quite shocked me, my dear. I was thinking it was one of our friends."

Lucinda merely rolled her wet eyes in reply and gave a loud sniff. She didn't have any friends. Mrs. Patton was only a hired companion; a widow with little money, noble birth, and no love of literature.

"Perhaps you need an airing, Lucinda," Mrs. Patton said in chipper voice as she stood. "We haven't been outside in three days. I'll call for a carriage. Why don't you get our calling cards? We can leave one at Mrs. Randall's house. A most advantageous social connection, indeed, especially considering her son is your father's business partner. Particularly when your own origins are more, shall we say, humble?"

"Humble," Lucinda echoed numbly and clutched the magazine to her chest.

Mrs. Patton and Lucinda sat in the carriage while the footman left calling cards at nine separate houses, including the Randalls'. For an airing, they weren't getting much air at all, and were instead just sitting like well-dressed dolls in a carriage. Lucinda still held the magazine against her chest, hoping somehow that she had misread it and the whole afternoon was only a terrible dream. But every time she flipped open the pages, the editor's note told her once again that Mrs. Smith was dead.

"Really, my dear," Mrs. Patton sighed, "you are not behaving like a well-brought-up young lady from Miss Holley's select school. It is foolish, and dare I add *unladylike,* to take so much to heart the death of a complete stranger."

"Yes, Mrs. Patton," Lucinda said and tried to chew on her thumbnail, only to remember she was wearing gloves.

But she was not a well-brought-up young lady—she was a stubborn one. And never knowing the ending to her favorite story was simply unacceptable.

Lucinda needed a plan. She would go to the editor and demand to be told everything he knew about Mrs. Smith. Surely one of Mrs. Smith's kin, or a particular friend, must know how she intended to finish the story. Or at the very least, they could allow Lucinda to peruse Mrs. Smith's notes and final papers. She opened the magazine and read the address on the cover page.

She was about to give the directions to her driver when a thought stopped her—*What if the editor refuses to see me?* The business district in London was run entirely by men. As much as it made Lucinda fume with indignation, an unchaperoned, unmarried young woman wouldn't make it past the front-desk clerk. If she wanted to be taken seriously by the editor, she would need a man to accompany her. It was preposterous nonsense, but Lucinda was willing to swallow her own pride in order to learn Eurydice's fate.

She knocked loudly on the side of the carriage. Mrs. Patton jerked her head in surprise as the carriage slowed to a stop. Lucinda leaned her head out of the open window and called, "Simms, please take us to my father's office on Tooley Street."

"Very good, miss," the coachman said, and tipped his hat to her.

Lucinda pulled her head back inside and said with a bright voice, "One more call to make today, Mrs. Patton."

"Just as you wish it, dear girl," Mrs. Patton said. "But keep in mind we have the party at the Freshams' tonight, and it would be wise for a young lady to rest before the exertions of dancing."

"I don't think I am in any danger of too much exertion walking from the carriage into my father's office."

Mrs. Patton sighed again and Lucinda ignored it. She had not been to her father's office in nearly four years, but before then, from the age of eight to the awkward age of fourteen, she'd spent nearly every day there. She'd played with dolls surrounded by the ledgers until her father started to give her little tasks to complete. The tasks grew more complicated over the years until she was faster at addition than any of his clerks and could catch a mistake in a number column better than even her father.

The carriage came to a stop, and Lucinda flung open the door and jumped out before the footman could assist her. The sign on the front of the imposing two-story brick building read RANDALL AND LEAVITT in bold black lettering.

Ignoring Mrs. Patton's calls for her to wait, Lucinda opened the door. Immediately she was met by the familiar smell of paper and leather-bound books. She breathed in deeply, inhaling memories. She did not bother to speak to any of the clerks; she knew her way around the office and didn't need—or want—them to escort her. Instead, she walked past row after row of desks, up the stairs, and down the hall to her father's office. She knocked on the door but did not wait for a reply before she opened it eagerly, only to find the room empty.

The room looked exactly the same as she remembered it. She caressed the well-worn desk with her fingers and then touched her father's wingback chair. She turned to see a familiar elderly man with snowy-white hair and black-beetle eyebrows standing behind her in the doorway.

"Excuse me, miss," he said. "May I be of assistance?"

"Mr. Murphy! How long it has been," Lucinda said. "How does your family?"

"My stars, it's Miss Lucy!"

"In the flesh," she said with her most winning smile. Miss Holley always said that a lady's greatest weapon was her smile.

"All grown up," he remarked kindly. "Mrs. Murphy will be so pleased that I saw you. She asked after you only last week. But I am afraid that your father has gone to his warehouse about some business."

"It is no great matter," Lucinda said. "I can wait in his office. I've learned that waiting is what ladies do best."

Another *invaluable* lesson from Miss Holley's Finishing School.

"And a fine lady you've turned out to be, Miss Lucy," Mr. Murphy said. "But your father might not return for several hours. If you need assistance, you should request it of Mr. Randall. He's in his father's old office, down the hall."

"I'd much rather not," Lucinda said, sitting in her father's wingback chair and tapping her fingers on his mahogany desk.

"Your father may not return to the office at all today, Miss Lucy," Mr. Murphy said anxiously. "I should hate to have you waste your entire afternoon. You'd better go speak to Mr. Randall."

Waiting and doing nothing was what Lucinda did every afternoon, but she did not wish to offend Mr. Murphy, who had always been so kind to her when she was younger. He'd often brought her cakes and cookies that his wife had made. But she cringed at the thought of having to ask Mr. David Randall for assistance. Even though he'd been her first—and only—friend.

David was the son of her father's business partner. She'd taught him how to read an accounting ledger, and he'd taught her how to play marbles and quoits. But then David's father died, leaving him—at only fifteen years old—owner of his father's half of the business. And then he was no longer her friend.

He was one of the reasons why she had been sent to a finishing school prison. She'd told him something in confidence, and he'd told his mother, who'd told her father, and Lucinda had found herself packed up and sent away to that ivied prison to become a lady. Just thinking of his self-satisfied face made Lucinda long to slap it.

Lucinda stood and exhaled. "Very well, Mr. Murphy. I will go and see if Mr. Randall will assist me."

She gave him a warm smile as she passed by and found that David's office door was already open. Unlike her father's office, which hadn't changed a whit in twenty years, this room had undergone a transformation. The shelves were lined with books instead of antique snuffboxes, and a large circular globe sat prominently on a much larger white oak desk. And behind it sat Mr. David Randall.

Lucinda fought the urge to roll her eyes; he was more handsome than she remembered. In the four years since she last saw him, his face had lost some of its youthfulness. Thick brown sideburns now ran down each side of his face, elongating his square jaw. His light brown eyes looked at her in surprise, and he stood up. He was one of the few men who were taller than Lucinda, at least six feet tall. It felt odd to look up to speak.

"Is there something I can help you with, ma'am—miss?" he asked in a pleasant tone.

He clearly didn't recognize her.

"I have never thought highly of your intelligence, Mr. Randall," Lucinda said, "but really, you should be able to remember your partner's only daughter."

Lucinda felt pleasure in seeing his eyes widen and his jaw

drop. She smiled and took a seat. She gestured for him to sit as well. He obeyed, perching on the edge of his chair like he was on a social call instead of sitting in his own office.

"There is something you can help me with since my father is not here," Lucinda said. His jaw dropped slightly lower. "Do not worry, it does not require any great effort on your part. I need you to accompany me to a publishing house and get me an appointment with the editor."

"A publishing house?"

"Yes, the place where they publish things," Lucinda said, as if he were a small child.

David did not respond immediately, but blinked at her as if he thought she was an apparition caused by the excessive heat.

"As much as I would like to assist you, Miss Leavitt," David said at last, "I am afraid that I have far too much work to do today."

He pointed to the stack of ledgers on his desk.

"I should not wish to keep you from your work." Lucinda turned in her seat to look at the door where Mr. Murphy was standing waiting patiently. "Mr. Murphy, would you be so good as to tell my coachman, Simms, to take Mrs. Patton home and then return here for me?"

Lucinda turned back to David as Mr. Murphy disappeared to do as she asked. She placed her magazine on his desk, then removed her gloves and bonnet. "Which one shall I start with?" she asked, smiling brightly.

He did not immediately reply, so Lucinda took the ledger from the top of the stack and picked up David's pen. She flipped to the last page and carefully began examining the columns, adding the numbers in her head.

"I have already done that one," David said as he pulled another pen out of his desk drawer and placed it on the ledger he'd been checking when she walked in.

"I know," Lucinda said, circling the third line over. "But you missed a mistake. The clerk is off a farthing in this column."

"Thank you, Miss Leavitt," David said dryly. "A quarter of a penny matters a great deal to our company's financial success."

Lucinda shrugged and muttered audibly, "It's still a mistake."

She handed the ledger back to David. He took it and then handed her another.

"I am grateful for your assistance," he said in a tone that sounded anything but thankful.

"I'm sure you are," she said. She loved numbers. She loved adding the impossibly high sums in her head with no other assistance but her mind. She checked the next ledger. Then the next. And finally, between the two of them, they had completed ten ledgers. She handed the last book back to David.

"I daresay, Simms has probably returned with the carriage by now," she said. "It is only a few blocks to my home and back. Shall we go to the publishing house?"

"The place that publishes things," David clarified with a small smile.

Lucinda wished to slap it from his face, but she was on her best behavior. So instead, she nodded and said, "Precisely."

Lucinda pulled on her gloves and bonnet, then picked up her magazine as David put on his coat and his tall beaver top hat.

She could not wipe the smug look off her face. She didn't even try to.

Two

DAVID RANDALL HATED RIDING BACKWARD in a carriage. It always made him feel sick. But he'd rather feel sick than sit next to Lucy—*Miss* Lucinda Leavitt now. Although sitting across from her gave him ample opportunity to view her alarming transformation from gangly girl to grown-up woman. He could hardly believe they were the same person. That is, until she opened her mouth; then David had no difficulty discerning his partner's outspoken daughter.

Gone was the stooped, overly tall girl with untidy braids. In her place was a woman who embraced all of her inches. Dark brown curls—nearly black—framed her oval face. She had large, startlingly light blue eyes with thick black lashes and brows. She was certainly an attractive young woman, but her expression was smug and self-satisfied.

David felt a twinge of annoyance. Lucinda's smug look reminded him of the expression on his father's face whenever he had made a mistake. His father had always made him feel foolish. Incapable.

"What is your business with the publisher?" David asked impatiently. "And, yes, I realize what a publisher is."

"I would love to gratify your idle curiosity, but I prefer to keep you in suspense," Lucinda said archly. "We require a few moments of the editor's time, a Mr. Thomas Gibbs."

David nodded and did not venture to speak again until they arrived at the offices of *Wheathill's Magazine*. The black building was tall and narrow, like a small book pressed between two larger ones, with a sign hanging above the door.

David waved aside the footman and hopped out of the carriage. He turned and offered his hand to Lucinda, who took it and carefully stepped down.

He could not help but notice that she smelled nice. Like flowers. David shook these irrelevant thoughts from his head and entered the building behind her. A bald clerk with thick sideburns gave a deferential nod to David and Lucinda.

David took out his business card and gave it to him. "I am Mr. David Randall, of Randall and Leavitt, and I require speech with your Mr. Thomas Gibbs immediately."

The clerk took the card and bowed again. "Yes, Mr. Randall. Just one moment, sir."

He disappeared through the door.

"Bravo," Lucinda said with a grin, and clapped her hands. "That was positively imperial."

Despite his efforts, David couldn't keep his lips from forming a small smile.

A few minutes later, the clerk returned with another gentleman. He was a head shorter than David, with red curly hair and even thicker sideburns than his clerk. The editor shook David's hand and then began to bow to Lucinda but stopped midway to ogle her. The editor must have realized he looked too long, because he straightened his posture and reddened right up to the roots of his hair.

"I am Mr. Thomas Gibbs. I assume I have the pleasure of addressing Mr. and Mrs. Randall?" he asked.

"No," Lucinda said. "I am Miss Leavitt. Mr. Randall is my father's business partner, and he kindly agreed to accompany me here. And I can assure you that the pleasure is all mine. I am a great admirer of your magazine, sir."

"Um, thank you."

"And I know a true connoisseur of literature like yourself would be only too ready to assist me in my quest to discover the true ending of Mrs. Smith's story."

David shook his head in disbelief, but Mr. Gibbs swallowed Lucinda's flattery like pear-drop candies.

"Of course," he said.

"Thank you so very much, Mr. Gibbs," she said. "Now, I would like the deceased Mrs. Smith's forwarding address, her first name if you know it, and the names of any surviving kin."

Mr. Gibbs's eyes widened, and he sputtered, "Ex-excuse me?"

Lucinda gave him a condescending smile. "Mrs. Smith, the author of *She Knew She Was Right*, the book you serialized in your magazine."

Mr. Gibbs blinked several times. "Of course, I would be only too happy to help you, Miss Leavitt. It is a pity the Lord took Mrs. Smith too soon."

"A great pity," Lucinda concurred. "Would you like to take us back to your office so you can retrieve the requested information?"

Gibbs blinked several more times. "Y-y-yes. This way, Miss Leavitt."

Gibbs opened the door for Lucinda and then followed her through it, allowing it to swing closed. David sighed. The fellow had forgotten his existence. He opened the door and found Lucinda leaning over the editor's desk. Gibbs flipped through a file, then took out a sheet of paper and handed it to her.

"We sent Mrs. Smith's last two payments to a Mrs. B. Smith staying in the boarding house at number fifteen Laura Place, Bath."

"Do you know what the *B* stands for?" Lucinda pressed.

"I'm afraid I do not," Gibbs said, shaking his red head. "No one in our office ever met her in person."

"I see," Lucinda said as she perused the paper again. "What address did you previously send her pay to?"

Gibbs riffled through the file for several minutes.

"My clerk must have misplaced it," Gibbs said at last.

"May I keep this paper?" Lucinda asked.

"Of course, Miss Leavitt," Gibbs said, his face reddening by the moment.

"And may I ask you another question, sir?"

"Anything."

David snorted.

Lucinda gave the editor a fulsome smile. "When was the last time you heard from Mrs. Smith?"

Gibbs riffled through the file one last time and pulled out a sheet of paper with the tiniest handwriting David had ever seen. "The last time I heard from her was in March, Miss Leavitt. Someone else sent these last two pages of the story, as well as a letter notifying me that Mrs. B. Smith had died."

He handed her the sheet of paper, and David leaned closer to hear Lucinda whisper underneath her breath:

"'My feelings are like a tangled web, Miss Emerson," Lord Dunstan said as he clasped her delicate hand between his two large ones. "And only you can unravel them.'"

She mumbled more lines that he could not understand before she said:

"'Miss Emerson," Mr. Thisbe said, "I believe that the Lord above ordained us for one another. Will you do me the great honor of becoming my wife?'"

"It's the last scene you published," Lucinda said as she looked up at Gibbs. "Who notified you of her death?"

The editor pulled another letter from the file, but the handwriting on this page was entirely different from the first. Each word was completed with a curvy flourish at the end, and the letter was one of the shortest he'd ever seen. Gibbs handed it to Lucinda and pointed to the bottom, which was conspicuously missing a signature.

"Here is the letter. Not signed, as you can see."

She shook her head and read aloud: "'*Mr. Gibbs, I regret to inform you that the author Mrs. B. Smith died on March 3, 1861, from an internal complaint. I've included the last pages that she gave for me to read. Yours.*' Unsigned. How very frustrating."

David pried both pages from Lucinda's fingers and handed them back to Gibbs. "Thank you for your help, Mr. Gibbs. If we require any additional assistance, we will let you know."

"Very good, sir," he said, and smiled as he added, "Miss Leavitt, it has been a very great pleasure making your acquaintance. It is a delight to meet a young lady who is as passionately fond of literature as yourself."

"You are too kind, Mr. Gibbs," Lucinda said, but her expression was forlorn.

David bowed to the editor, then took Lucinda by the elbow and escorted her out of the building. She did not pull away, but walked as if she were dazed. David handed her into the carriage and then nodded to Gibbs, who had followed them to the front door. He tapped his cane against the side of the carriage to signal the coachman to drive.

"That was rather abrupt, Mr. Randall," Lucinda said, rubbing her elbow. "What is your hurry?"

David rolled his eyes. "I have real work to do, and I could not stand to listen to him fawn over you any longer. Why did you encourage him?"

"Why shouldn't I encourage a man of comfortable circumstances to compliment me?" Lucinda asked, back to her sharp self. "Is it not a young woman's purpose in life to find a suitable man to marry her, and take on all of the worldly cares that are too difficult for her delicate constitution?"

"Yours is anything but delicate," he retorted, knowing full well she was needling him.

"Well, you should know," Lucinda said. "We've been acquainted since childhood and I have not altered."

"In some ways, you haven't," he said, looking her up and down. "And in others, you most definitely have."

"And you haven't changed one bit," she said, folding her arms across the silly magazine that she'd carried around all day like a doll.

"Thank you."

"It wasn't meant to be a compliment."

"I am aware of that."

Lucinda pursed her lips and eyed him with a fastidiousness that made him squirm beneath her gaze. After moments of contemplation, she finally said, "Shall I drop you off at the office or shall I take you home?"

"The office is fine, Miss Leavitt."

She did not speak again until the carriage pulled up in front of the red brick building. He exited the carriage and turned to tip his hat to her. She nodded and said, "Good day, Mr. Randall. Thank you for your assistance with the publishing house."

"The place that publishes things," he said gravely and bowed to her, then turned to enter the countinghouse, not waiting for nor wanting to see her reaction.

Back upstairs in his office, he found that enough work for three men had been left on his desk. David sighed, taking off his hat and untying his cravat. He needed more air and more time.

Three

"HOW WAS THE OFFICE TODAY, Father?" Lucinda asked as she sipped a spoonful of mock turtle soup.

"Adequate," her father said, not bothering to look up at her from his own bowl. He continued eating as if Lucinda and Mrs. Patton were not even in the room.

Mrs. Patton raised her eyebrows and said in a chipper voice, "Lucinda and I had a wonderful day. We finished embroidering the most beautiful cushion, did we not?"

"Oh, we did," Lucinda said with false enthusiasm. "*All* afternoon."

"And Mrs. Randall left her calling card," Mrs. Patton continued. "I had hoped she would actually come in and visit, but she didn't."

"I wish she had as well," Lucinda said. "I've never actually seen Mrs. Randall. I am not sure I believe she really exists. Have you seen her, Father?"

He glanced up from his bowl of soup, but did not look at Lucinda. "I have had the pleasure of dining with her and Mr. Randall at least a half dozen times. And I can assure you that she does indeed exist."

A half dozen dinners in more than twenty years of doing business with their family did not seem like many to Lucinda.

"I have also seen Mrs. Randall at a party," Mrs. Patton added. "But I didn't make her acquaintance there. It was such a crush, the house so full of guests, all from the very best families."

Neither Lucinda nor her father responded to this remark, leaving an awkward silence around the table. Lucinda's lineage was anything but noble. Her father began life as a street sweeper, and through his natural talent with numbers and hard work found a place as a clerk in a countinghouse. Her mother had been a nursery maid to a middle-class family in Kensington before she married her father. But her mother had wasted away from consumption when Lucinda was only eight years old, and her father never truly recovered from it. He removed everything that reminded him of his wife—her portrait, her embroidery, their furniture—and he and Lucinda moved to a new house. He threw himself entirely into his work and rose to a partnership in the same countinghouse. Then David betrayed her confidence, and Lucinda began to resemble her mother too much for her father's comfort, so she was sent away to school. As if she were just another dispensable reminder of something he'd lost.

The awkward silence was broken when Mr. Ruffles and the first footman took away their soup bowls and set out plates for the next courses: pheasant, oyster pâté, lamb cutlets, asparagus, bread au jus, and a roast saddle of mutton. The dining room was soon entirely silent except for the scraping of silverware on plates.

Lucinda slowly chewed her bite of oyster. Before she'd gone to finishing school, dinners had been much more casual affairs. They didn't change their clothes, and they never ate in the formal dining room, but rather in the much smaller breakfast room. And she and her father had talked—*really* talked—about things that mattered to him. Mostly about his countinghouse, because his work filled his entire life.

A life that grown-up Lucinda no longer seemed to fit into.

Once they were finished with the main course, Mr. Ruffles and the footman removed their plates and the tablecloth, then served champagne and a pudding for dessert. Desserts always made her think of her mother—she had loved dessert. Chocolate mousse was her very favorite dish. Lucinda wished for the thousandth time that her mother were still alive. Still with them.

But all she had left of her mother was a small cameo brooch likeness of her. She'd kept it hidden from her father all these years. Even as a child, she'd been afraid he would take it and consign it to the attic with her mother's portrait, to gather dust and be forgotten. But Lucinda hadn't forgotten her mother, even if she couldn't remember the exact details of her face. She remembered how loved she always felt when her mother looked at her. And how much she wanted to feel that love now.

"I was wondering if I might, perhaps, have my mother's portrait to hang in my bedroom?" she asked, taking a sip of champagne. "It is only gathering dust in the attic, after all."

"No," her father said.

Lucinda swallowed and pressed on. "But if I keep it in my bedroom, you won't have to see it . . . and I have almost forgotten what she looks like—"

He stood abruptly and dropped his napkin on the table.

"Where are you going, Father?" Lucinda asked, rising from her seat.

He didn't look at her. He never looked at her.

"To my study," he said. "I have work to do."

"But it's nearly nine o'clock."

"Excellent," Mrs. Patton said, standing. She grabbed Lucinda's elbow and steered her away from her father. "Lucinda and I shall adjourn to the sitting room for some coffee."

"But I—" Lucinda started to protest, but her father was already gone. Mutely, she allowed herself to be guided by the much shorter—and yet surprisingly strong-gripped—Mrs. Patton to the sitting room, where she dutifully and dully drank her coffee.

The next day Lucinda ran her pen down the column of her household accounts. Every farthing was accounted for. Naturally.

The sitting room faced west, and the heat of the afternoon blared through the three large windows that faced the London street. Lucinda tapped her pen against the table impatiently. Her mathematical mind was wasted on simple household accounts. The repetitious inanity of it all!

Lucinda needed something to occupy her time. She picked up a sheet of paper and touched the end of her pen to her lips before writing:

No. 15 Laura Place, Bath
To the Owner of the Establishment:

I am writing to request any forwarding information on a guest, Mrs. B. Smith, who you had staying in your boardinghouse from January to February of this year. I am trying to locate her family or nearest relations on important business. I have enclosed a fresh sheet of paper and a penny stamp, so replying to my letter will not cost you a farthing. I appreciate your time and attention in this matter.

Yours sincerely,
L. Leavitt
London

Lucinda poured a little sand on the letter to help dry the ink and then blew it off. She picked up a second sheet of paper and folded it inside the first, then placed a penny stamp inside the letter and sealed it with wax. She waited for the wax to firmly dry before turning the letter over and addressing it, and then she pulled the cord for a servant. Mr. Ruffles came into the room with a bow.

Lucinda handed him the letter. "Please see that this letter leaves with today's post," she said.

"Yes, miss."

"Thank you, Ruffles," Lucinda said. Across the sitting room, Mrs. Patton was snoring ever so slightly, her head hung to one side and her mouth agape. Mr. Ruffles looked at the sleeping companion and shook his square head in distaste before bowing to Lucinda once more and leaving the room.

A week later, Lucinda had yet to hear back from the proprietor in Bath about Mrs. Smith. She dabbed the sweat from her brow with a handkerchief and noticed the door to her father's study was ajar. She carefully eased the door open farther so her enormous skirt could fit through. Lucinda closed the door behind her and walked over to sit in her father's chair.

On the desk was a large stack of ledgers. She opened the first one and ran her finger down the column of numbers. She dipped the pen in the inkwell and put a checkmark at the bottom of the column. And then the next one. And then a third.

She found a few petty errors—which she corrected—but nothing substantial.

Finally she opened the last ledger—a Mr. Quill's from the Bath office. The first eight pages were flawlessly perfect, but the ninth page was perplexing. The beginning numbers did not match the ending numbers on the eighth page. The ninth page was added correctly, as were the twenty pages after it. But between the eighth page and the ninth page, twenty-three pounds had simply disappeared.

Lucinda bit what was left of her thumbnail. Perhaps a page had fallen out? She turned the ledger over in her hands, but it looked brand new, the binding clearly intact. Had the clerk simply forgotten to carry over a few numerals? Lucinda doubled-checked her math, but surely not even the greenest of apprentices in her father's employ could make such a blatant error and not notice. There were no two ways about it: Mr. Quill was an embezzler.

Lucinda stood excitedly. She could show her father this ledger and prove she was clever enough to work in his countinghouse. That she was capable of so much more than her current banal existence of embroidery and endless sitting.

She tucked Mr. Quill's ledger underneath her arm and tiptoed out of the office. Mrs. Patton was lying on the sofa, fast asleep. Lucinda quietly left the sitting room and asked Mr. Ruffles to call for her carriage. She carefully placed the ledger into her embroidery bag—which finally had a *useful* purpose.

When Lucinda arrived at the countinghouse, all the windows were open but the heat was just as unbearable there as it had been at home. She walked past the clerks, who were mopping their sweaty brows with handkerchiefs, and went upstairs, where she opened the door to her father's office without knocking. Her father looked so slight sitting in the large wingback chair at his desk. The top of his head was bald and shiny with sweat, a gray band of hair surrounding it. His beard and mustache were the same iron gray of his hair. His long, thin fingers gripped his pen tightly as he wrote a letter. Lucinda did not wait for him to greet her before entering the room.

"Hello, Father," she said gaily.

He glanced up at her, but his eyes immediately dropped back down to the letter he was writing. "Lucy, what are you doing here?"

"I was hoping I might be able to assist you," Lucinda said. "I found some ledgers at home and I checked them. There were only a few petty mistakes, until—"

Her father shook his bald, shiny head back and forth, still not looking her in the eye. "Ledgers are not for young ladies, Lucy."

"Then I could help you with your letters, Father," Lucinda pressed, touching the stack of letters on his desk. "You had me open and file letters when I was only a little girl. Surely I could be more helpful now that I am eighteen."

He stood, though he was several inches shorter than her. "Your mother wanted you to be a lady, and a lady is what you will be."

"But—"

"No buts," he said, raising his right hand. "This conversation is nonnegotiable. There will be no more looking through ledgers at home and no more visits to the countinghouse. Do you understand?"

"I understand, but I don't agree," Lucinda muttered.

"You don't have to agree," he said. "Now, shall I escort you back home?"

"No need, Father," Lucinda said, and then lied, "Mrs. Patton is waiting in the carriage. I will shut the door behind me."

Lucinda pressed the door closed and leaned back against it, exhaling slowly. She looked at the floor and breathed in and out several times. She wanted to yell in rage and frustration at the unfairness of it all, but she didn't. If there was one thing she had learned from finishing school, it was to keep everything bottled up inside. Arguing had only ever earned her stripes from the strap and enforced isolation in the attic. She continued to breathe slowly in and out until she dropped her embroidery bag on the floor and heard a clunk.

Mr. Quill's ledger was still inside of it. Her father had never given her the opportunity to tell him about the embezzler. She looked down the hall and saw that David's office door was open again. *Probably for the circulation of air,* she thought.

Lucinda lifted her head and walked resolutely to David's office. She knocked lightly on the open door.

David sat at his desk with his cravat untied and the top of his linen shirt open. His vest and jacket were hung on the coatrack in the corner. She could see a bead of sweat on his exposed collarbone. The slight breeze from the windows behind him stirred his hair. He did not look up but continued to write a letter; he must not have heard her knock.

Lucinda took a few steps forward and cleared her throat.

David glanced up at her and shot to his feet in surprise. Or attempted to. He'd forgotten to push out his chair first, so instead, the tops of his knees slammed into his desk, and he nearly toppled back into his chair before he managed to stand. He gave her a stiff bow and then clutched at the opening at the top of his shirt.

"Lucy—Miss Leavitt, how do you do?"

Lucinda grinned; she'd never seen the perfect Mr. David Randall so disheveled. She pointed to the chair and said primly, "May I sit, please?"

"Yes, of course," he said. He hastily buttoned up his shirt, one button off of the correct one.

Lucinda sat. After a moment she said coyly, "Must you tower over me?"

He dropped into his chair instantly and then looked over his shoulder for his vest and coat. He stood again as if to go retrieve them.

"There's no need," Lucinda said. "It's hot enough already."

David smiled at her, and inexplicably she felt hotter. He sat back down, rested his elbows on his desk, and interlaced his fingers. "What can I help you with today, Miss Leavitt?"

"Why do you assume I need your assistance?"

"I can think of no other reason for you to be here in my office."

Lucinda let out a tinkle of laughter. "I am not here for your assistance, but rather to offer you mine."

"What assistance?"

She pulled Mr. Quill's ledger out of her embroidery bag and handed it to David. "My father had me go over some of the ledgers at our home, and I found one I think you ought to look at."

He opened it and looked at the first couple pages. "What's wrong with it?"

"The numbers between pages eight and nine are not consecutive," Lucinda said. "Somehow between the two pages, twenty-three pounds disappeared into thin air."

David turned a few more pages and then looked back and forth from page eight to page nine. "You are right."

"My father would like us both to go to the Bath office and perform an audit on all the books," Lucinda continued quickly, careful not to look him in the eye. It was easier to lie if you didn't maintain eye contact. Another *invaluable* lesson from finishing school. "You'll probably want to contact the justice of the peace about Mr. Quill while we are there."

"I do not see why you need to come," David said slowly.

"Don't you want my help?" Lucinda asked. "I'm much faster at numbers than you."

"That's true," David admitted. "But I can't help but think you only wish to perform the Bath audit so you may visit Laura

Street and inquire after your dead author. And I am very busy at the moment." He gestured to the stack of letters on his desk.

"I have underrated your intelligence, David," Lucinda said, forgetting to be formal in her excitement. She untied her bonnet and took it off. "But I do believe the Bath audit is truly essential. And if we are, by happy coincidence, already in Bath, what could it hurt to take a brief trip to Laura Street to make an inquiry? And, if we hurry, we can finish all the correspondence on your desk and set out for Bath on the earliest train tomorrow. I should not think we need stay there for more than a night. Be sure to have your man pack the appropriate clothes."

"I cannot escort you to Bath—"

"Without a chaperone," Lucinda finished. "Mrs. Patton would love to visit Bath and drink the waters. The poor dear's health seems quite precarious; she falls asleep at the least provocation."

David exhaled loudly.

"Which stack of letters shall I start on?" Lucinda asked brightly.

Lucinda stood perfectly still as her lady's maid dressed her in a blue taffeta gown for dinner. She felt like a doll as her maid moved her arms up and down and buttoned the back of her dress. The maid curled the hair around Lucinda's face and intertwined a matching blue ribbon through her locks. Then, she expertly applied carmine on Lucinda's lips and rice powder on her face. Lucinda stuck her tongue out at her reflection in the mirror—she truly looked like a white-faced porcelain doll.

But when she went down to dinner, she wore her best weapon—her smile. Lucinda nodded politely at all of Mrs. Patton's ramblings during the first three courses.

"I had my own horse when I was a young lady, named Nebuchadnezzar," Mrs. Patton said. "A neatish brown mare with the most excellent of manners."

"It is a pity Nebuchadnezzar isn't still alive," Lucinda said as she picked up her wineglass. "With his excellent manners, we could have invited him to dinner. I am sure he would have enlivened the conversation."

She sipped her wine while Mrs. Patton laughed and her father even smiled.

"My dear Lucinda," Mrs. Patton said. "You know, you can really be charming when you wish to be."

"Dear Nebuchadnezzar reminds me of something that happened at finishing school," Lucinda said, setting her glass back on the table. "Miss Ursula Atkinson put horse manure on her face because Miss Clara Hardin told her it would rid her of her freckles."

"Oh, dear!" Mrs. Patton said with a high-pitched laugh.

"I assume it did not," her father said dryly.

"It did rid her of something."

"What?" Mrs. Patton asked.

"Companions," Lucinda said. "The poor girl smelled awful for a week and never lived it down."

Her father laughed. It was the first time she'd heard him laugh in nearly four years. It was extremely loud and jolly. Miss Clara Hardin would have called it vulgar. Lucinda loved the sound of it. She could tell he was pleased. She was behaving like the sweet society debutante he wanted her to be.

"Father," Lucinda said, sensing her opportunity. "Another schoolfellow, Miss Amelia Butterfield, told me of a lacemaker in Bath that makes the most exquisite point lace. It would be the perfect trimming for my scarlet evening gown, and I want to look my very best at my first dinner party next week. It is terribly important that I make a good impression. Please say Mrs. Patton and I may go to Bath to purchase some point lace? Please, Father?"

He stroked his chin. "Bath seems an awfully long way to go for lace."

"Lacemaking is an art form," Mrs. Patton said, coming to Lucinda's aid. "A truly gifted tatter is worth seeking out whatever the distance."

"And Mrs. Patton and I could drink from the waters of Bath," Lucinda added quickly, surprised Mrs. Patton had supported the idea so easily. "It has been so hot and I have been feeling quite poorly, which has caused me to behave in an unladylike manner. I believe drinking the waters of Bath would be just the thing to set us both up. Don't you agree, Mrs. Patton?"

"I have drank the waters of Bath before and found them to be greatly beneficial," Mrs. Patton said. "I was a lady's companion to Lady Louisa Moulton then. Such a dear girl. She made a very good match to Viscount Etters."

"Please, *Papa*," Lucinda begged, using the name that she'd called him as a child. It was the ace in her hand, and she played it with precision.

"I suppose—" he began.

"Excellent," Lucinda said, cutting him off. "Mr. Randall is traveling to Bath tomorrow, and he can accompany us."

"Mr. Randall would be an excellent escort," her father said.

"How do you know that, Lucinda?" Mrs. Patton asked.

Lucinda's eyes darted from Mrs. Patton's suspicious ones to her father's shrewd ones. "My dear Mrs. Patton, I forgot to tell you. *Mrs.* Randall paid us a call this afternoon and told me all about it. I almost woke you, but you were sleeping so soundly that I didn't."

Her father's sharp eyes turned from studying Lucinda to evaluating Mrs. Patton. She saw the older woman's color heighten as she sat up even straighter in her chair.

"In the future, always wake me, Lucinda," she said, attempting to retrieve her slipping dignity. "I am not only your companion, but your chaperone. It is vital for your social importance to have me present when you have visitors."

"I did not know," Lucinda said as innocently as she could. She lowered her eyes as she added, "I am so sorry. It will not happen again."

“I should not have been sleeping,” Mrs. Patton said. Then fanned herself and added, “But this heat is so oppressive.”

Lucinda stood. “I will go have the maid pack my things. We have an early train to catch tomorrow.”

She left the dining room still in the character of an elegant young lady, but when she reached the stairs, she climbed them by twos. And once in her room, she jumped up and down and squealed silently. Tomorrow, she would escape her prison.

Four

MRS. PATTON YAWNED WIDELY AS THEY stood at the entrance of Paddington Station. Lucinda pulled out her pocket watch and looked at the time: It was half past eight. If David didn't hurry, they would miss the first train.

As if he'd heard her anxious thoughts, David stepped out of a two-wheeled hansom cab with a small portmanteau. He paid the driver and strode purposefully toward them with his broad shoulders back and his head held high.

"There you are, David," Lucinda said with a wave of her hand. "Allow me to introduce my chaperone and companion, Mrs. Patton."

He touched his gloved hand to the rim of his top hat.

Mrs. Patton, for once, was wide awake and gave him an enormous smile and curtsy. *He isn't that handsome,* Lucinda thought with annoyance.

"Mr. Randall, please accept my apologies for my charge addressing you so informally," Mrs. Patton simpered. "Lucinda, a lady never calls a gentleman by his given name unless they are closely related family members."

"Very well," Lucinda said. "*Mr.* Randall, will you please help us with our luggage?"

"Are both of those yours?" David asked, pointing to their two sizable trunks.

"Yes."

"We are only going for one night."

"I know, or else we would have had to bring *four* trunks," Lucinda said brightly. "Being a lady requires a great deal of baggage, does it not, Mrs. Patton?"

"Yes, yes it does," Mrs. Patton agreed emphatically.

David shook his head bemusedly. "I'll get a porter."

"Not strong enough to carry them yourself?" Lucinda asked teasingly.

"Not stupid enough," David retorted. He returned in less than a minute with a porter dressed all in blue, pushing a trolley. The porter loaded the two heavy trunks onto the trolley and led the way to the platform where they would board the train. Lucinda walked beside David as Mrs. Patton endeavored to keep up.

A conductor opened the door to the first-class train car

for them. David handed Lucinda in and then Mrs. Patton. They found an empty compartment, where Lucinda chose the seat facing forward, and Mrs. Patton sat beside her. The porter secured their luggage, and David tossed the man a coin before entering the compartment and sitting across from the ladies.

A short time later, the train lurched forward and began to rattle over the tracks. The gentle movement soon had Mrs. Patton right to sleep, her head hanging forward. Lucinda looked at her other traveling companion and saw that David appeared rather pale.

"Are you feeling sick?"

"No," David said, covering his mouth and nose with a handkerchief.

Lucinda stood and sat back down next to him. She touched his arm in concern. His eyes were closed, and he seemed to be concentrating.

"What can I do to help you?"

"I'm fine," David said, opening his light brown eyes. "I just get a little unwell when I travel sitting backward."

"Why did you not say so before, Dav—Mr. Randall? You silly man," Lucinda chided. "Take my seat and I will sit over here."

David did not immediately move, so Lucinda gave him a slight shove with the hand she had rested on his arm. Reluctantly, he moved to the opposite seat. He did not speak for several minutes, but his color returned to normal—not that Lucinda was looking. But she happened to notice it between enjoying the scenery that whizzed past the train.

"I don't mind if you call me David, as you did when we were children," he said at last.

"You may *not* call me Lucy, as you did when we were children."

He blinked in surprise.

She gave him a saucy smile and tipped her head forward. "You may call me Lucinda."

"Lu-*cin*-da," he said slowly, as if he were tasting each syllable. Then he nodded toward Mrs. Patton's gently snoring form. "Does she always sleep this much?"

"Yes," Lucinda said. "If she sits down, she falls right to sleep."

"A sleeping chaperone is hardly an ideal one."

"Depends on your perspective," Lucinda said. "A sleeping chaperone can be a perfect one if you do not want them overly involved in your every moment. *You* would not be able to endure any chaperone at all."

"True," David said. "But I am not a young, unmarried woman."

"One would think with a woman on the throne, that women in England would have more freedom," Lucinda said. "If anything, it is less. Miss Holley—the lady who ran the finishing school I attended—told me that when she was a girl, ladies were allowed to go on carriage rides alone with young men. Now if a lady were to do that, her reputation would be ruined."

"Is there a particular young man you have in mind?"

"No," Lucinda answered honestly. "I should like to ride around in a carriage all by myself. I just wish young women were granted the same privileges as young men. The same opportunities for education and business."

"I was wondering when we were going to get to business," David said with a sympathetic smile. "But you are fortunate in your father. He is allowing you to be a part of his business."

Lucinda had the grace to blush. She had no intention of disabusing David of his belief that her father was supportive of her helping at the countinghouse.

"Odd, isn't it?" Lucinda said. "You left school to join the business, and soon after, I left the business to go to school. Do you regret not finishing your courses at Eton?"

David shook his head slowly. "I have regretted far more that my father did not teach me anything practical relating to his business affairs. Whenever I tried to help, he sent me away like a pesky child. And at Eton, I studied the classics and natural sciences. Neither of which have proved particularly useful in my employment."

"I daresay they are still more useful in your life than courses on needlework and music," Lucinda countered.

"You forgot deportment."

"How could I?" Lucinda said. "I was hit on the back with a strap until I learned to sit up straight and walk with my head up."

Subconsciously, Lucinda brought her hand to her neck and

shoulder, remembering all the many times she'd been struck for slouching. She had slouched because she was so tall and did not want to bring more attention to herself and her height. The meanest teacher, Miss Tenney, wasted no opportunity to punish Lucinda for every slight infraction.

Lucinda met David's eyes. He must have realized he had conjured a painful memory, for he tried to change the subject. "And drawing. Don't all refined young ladies draw?"

"Alas, I have no talent for drawing," Lucinda admitted. "Or music either. Although no effort was spared to teach me the rudimentary knowledge of the pianoforte. I have learned by heart three pieces of music should I ever be requested to play."

"It is too bad you cannot display your mathematical skills," David said. "Members of the audience could call out two numbers and you could tell them what they added up to."

"They would need to call out at least three numbers," Lucinda countered, "so that I would be slightly challenged."

David nodded at this, then turned toward the window. Lucinda resolutely stared out the window on the other side. They passed several farms and could see a few villages in the distance. Mrs. Patton continued to snore. Lucinda glanced again at David who was, to her surprise, watching her intently.

"I am sorry you were treated harshly at finishing school," he said. "I had no idea they treated girls like that. The strap was used quite freely at Eton as well. . . . When I told my mother what you confided to me, I did not know she would tell your father to send you to school."

"What did you expect?"

David's face flushed red. "That she would explain to you about a woman's menses. About the changes that were happening to your person."

"I thought I was dying," Lucinda said at last. "I am grateful that you at least assured me I wasn't."

"I was a fifteen-year-old boy, hardly an ideal person to explain such things to a fourteen-year-old girl," David said, the exasperation clear in his voice. "And I thought you would be more comfortable hearing about it from another woman."

"And I thought my only friend was trying to get rid of me," Lucinda said. "Out of the office. Out of his life."

"I wasn't trying to get you out of the office or out of my life," David said. "I was only trying to help you, like you helped me when my father died. You were the one who taught me all the different aspects of the business. I would have been sunk without you, despite your father's patience. And as I said before, I was only trying to help you."

"Next time *ask* me how I would like to be helped," Lucinda said, much louder than she had meant to.

Mrs. Patton stirred. "Oh dear, I must have dozed," she said. "How long to Bath?"

"I will go ask the conductor," David said, and abruptly left the compartment.

Mrs. Patton looked from David's departing figure to Lucinda sitting on the opposite seat.

"Lucinda, pray, why are you sitting over there?"

"Mr. Randall was feeling sick riding backward."

Mrs. Patton nodded. "Well, I suppose I had better switch sides as well. I am your chaperone, after all."

Mrs. Patton awkwardly got out of the seat and plunked down next to Lucinda. David returned after a few minutes and said the trip should be over within half an hour. Mrs. Patton thanked him cordially and even managed to stay awake until they reached the train station in Bath.

Five

DAVID FELT A WEIGHT FALL from him as the train came to a stop and they began to disembark. Being with Lucinda was equal parts exhilarating and exhausting.

After they left the train and hailed a hackney coach, they stopped briefly to drop off their luggage at the Pelican Inn, a respectable hotel only a street away from the Pump Room and Bath Abbey. Then, the coach continued on until it pulled up in front of a white-stone building. David assisted Lucinda out of the vehicle, followed by Mrs. Patton.

"This is not a lace shop," Mrs. Patton said in surprise.

"Mrs. Patton," Lucinda said, touching the older woman's arm. "Do you not remember when my father mentioned it last night?"

"I do not."

"You must have dozed off during that bit," Lucinda said. "My father needs me to assist Mr. Randall in an audit of the Bath office. But I assure you we won't be long. Will we, Mr. Randall?"

"We will accomplish the audit as quickly as possible," he said, holding open the door to the office for the ladies. He followed leisurely behind them.

Inside there were ten clerks at their own individual desks, all looking agog at Lucinda. She smiled. "May I speak to the manager, Mr. Baxter, please?"

All ten clerks shuffled to their feet. The clerk sitting closest to her stood so quickly that he bumped over his bottle of ink. He righted the bottle and then offered his arm in a grandiose manner to Lucinda. To David's surprise, she offered the pimply fellow a wide smile and took his arm. He led her up the staircase to the upper office. David found Mrs. Patton holding on to his arm as she breathed heavily mounting each stair. They stepped up from the stairs to a small landing in front of a red door with a glass window.

The pimply clerk opened the door with a great flourish and said in a grand manner, "Mr. Baxter, you have guests."

David had met Mr. Baxter before, two years previous, and the man looked precisely the same. He had small, watery blue eyes, a large nose, and an enormous black beard and side-burns. He stood up when he saw the ladies; he was at least a head shorter than Lucinda and had a large round belly. He put his thumbs into his vest pockets and said genially, "Now, ladies, to what do we owe the pleasure of this visit?"

David stepped from behind Mrs. Patton. "I'm Mr. David Randall, as I'm sure you recall. This is Miss Leavitt. She wished to inspect the Bath office's books."

Mr. Baxter's small eyes widened at this, and he bowed obsequiously to David. "Mr. Randall, come right into my office. Such a pleasure to have you here. Is there anything I can get for you? Some tea? Refreshments?"

Mrs. Patton found her voice. "Tea and refreshments would be most appreciated, sir."

Mr. Baxter gave her what may have been called a charming smile and ushered the older lady to a soft chair. Lucinda found her own seat and David sat down beside her. The office was not large and felt a trifle crowded with four occupants.

Mr. Baxter stood behind his desk. "How can I be of assistance today?" he asked.

Before David could speak, Lucinda said brightly, "We shall need the last six months of ledgers. Possibly more, but we will start with those."

"I will have a clerk bring them immediately," Mr. Baxter said.

He had moved to leave the office when Lucinda added, "Would it be a terrible inconvenience if Mr. Randall and myself had sole use of your office for this afternoon?"

Mr. Baxter's round belly hit the doorframe as he turned around to reassure her that he would be most happy to accommodate her. Then he left to summon a clerk for the ledgers.

Lucinda took off her gloves and then her bonnet. Her dark brown hair was a comely mess of curls. She patted it with her hands, but only succeeded in making it worse. She seemed to realize this, for she began to take out all the hairpins. Her hair cascaded down her back in dark waves.

"My dear girl," Mrs. Patton said, "it is hardly appropriate to have your hair down in front of a gentleman."

Lucinda smirked. "I can assure you that Mr. Randall is made of sterner stuff than that. But if the sight of my hair down does indeed cause him to swoon, I promise to catch him before he hits the floor."

David laughed so loudly that he missed part of Mrs. Patton's apology for her charge's "lively manners." Meanwhile, Lucinda twisted her hair into a large bun at the bottom of her neck. She stabbed the bun ruthlessly with the pins until it stayed. She was looking rather . . . presentable when Mr. Baxter and two clerks returned to the room. The pimply clerk carried a tray with a teapot, three glasses, three plates, a cake, three forks, and a knife. The other clerk was a husky middle-aged man who easily carried a large stack of ledgers. Mr. Baxter directed both clerks to set their encumbrances on his desk, and then he bowed his leave of them.

Mrs. Patton—with a speed that belied her age—went to the desk and poured three cups of tea and sliced three generous pieces of cake.

"Lucinda," she said, "please give Mr. Randall his tea and cake."

Lucinda, for once, did as she was told and delivered the refreshments to David. Her hand brushed his as she placed the cup of tea in his hand; David thought her skin felt surprisingly soft. She returned to the desk for her own, and they all sat in companionable silence while they ate. Lucinda was the first to finish eating, and she immediately made herself comfortable in Mr. Baxter's chair behind his desk. She picked up the first ledger and set to work with a dedication that none of David's employees ever reached.

David leisurely finished eating his cake. Mrs. Patton did not leave even a crumb on her plate and then promptly dozed in her chair. David took off his hat and ran his fingers through his hair; he was already starting to sweat from the heat of the day. He glanced at Lucinda, whose eyes were on him.

"Admiring me, Lucinda?"

"What could there possibly be for me to admire, David?" she said lightly, but her face was flushed and David was positive that it was not caused by the heat of the day.

"Plenty," David said, and winked theatrically at her.

Lucinda bit her lower lip to prevent a smile and shook her head. She did not look up at him again, but instead focused on the ledger in front of her with renewed dedication. David leisurely picked up the next ledger on the stack and began to glance through it, looking for numerical discrepancies. He methodically checked the addition and the subtraction. He was not as mathematically gifted as Lucinda, or her father, both of whom could look at a column and come up with the sum in a matter of seconds.

They continued to work for over an hour in complete silence, save for Mrs. Patton's snores. Each ledger David examined was perfectly in order, much to his growing frustration. He was hot, and this audit was a waste of his time. He dropped the ledger onto the desk, and Lucinda looked up at the noise.

"I believe we are finished," he said. "Everything is in order. Baxter can dismiss Quill and we are done with this business."

Lucinda must not have liked craning her neck to look up at him, for she stood. "I only need another hour. Surely since we have come all this way, you can spare me one more hour?"

"Have you found anything substantial?" he asked.

Lucinda bit her lip again, and this time it was not to hide a smile. She shook her head slightly. "Something just doesn't feel right."

"Your woman's intuition?"

"My business sense," she countered. Her hands were clenched into tight fists as if she were ready to challenge him to a bout of fisticuffs if he refused her. If Lucinda felt *that* strongly about staying . . . he could certainly honor her request.

"What is another hour of my time?" David said finally. "Besides, it would be most uncivil of us to wake Mrs. Patton from her nap."

Lucinda laughed and gave him a genuine smile. This

smile was pure light, and for the first time since her return from school, David could see the girl he had once known.

And that was when he realized how closely he was standing to her—close enough to feel her sweet breath on his face. Close enough to embrace her.

He cleared his throat and stepped back, bumping a ledger off the desk. It hit the floor with a clatter. Mrs. Patton sat up ramrod straight and said, as if she had never been asleep, "Yes, this is quite a snug little office."

Lucinda took a step back. Had she been leaning toward him? "Isn't it just?" she managed.

David stooped down and picked up the dropped ledger, which turned out to be Mr. Baxter's personal one. It had fallen open, and he examined the revealed page as he brought it back to the desk. He ran his finger over the final column, then compared it to the same page in the ledger Lucinda had been checking. The numbers in the clerk's ledgers were not right. It was impossible for the numbers of the entire office and the individual records to be so discordant.

He pointed to the final numbers. "Miss Leavitt, what do you make of this?"

Lucinda stepped closer to him and bent her head next to his. As she did so, he caught the faintest scent of flowers. She peered at the ledger with her singleness of purpose.

"There is nothing wrong with the other clerks' ledgers," she said at last, "because they started with false numbers. Fetch a paper and we will compare the real numbers to the false ones."

David found a sheet of hot press paper, sat at the desk, and picked up a pen. Lucinda read him row after row of numbers from Baxter's ledger and then the numbers that were written in each individual clerk's book. David carefully kept the numbers in corresponding rows. After Lucinda read the last one and David wrote it down, he said, "Give me a moment to total it all."

"No need," Lucinda said from over his shoulder. "The difference is four hundred twenty-seven pounds, six shillings, and four pence."

David whistled softly. "That is a sizable amount of money."

"A small fortune," Lucinda agreed.

"Shocking," Mrs. Patton added, "just shocking."

"What are we going to do now?" Lucinda asked, putting her hand on his shoulder.

David tried not to notice how much her touch affected him. He stood up rather abruptly. "I shall take you and Mrs. Patton to the hotel, and then I will return here with a constable."

"I should like to stay," Lucinda said, folding her arms across her chest in resolute defiance.

"It might not be safe," he said. "Baxter is a strong man, and he might try to do something rash."

"We should heed Mr. Randall's advice, Lucinda," Mrs. Patton said as she stood and moved toward the door. "And besides, a business is no place for a lady."

He saw Lucinda's jaw tighten and her lips purse together at these words. Baxter was not the only one who wouldn't back down without a fight. "Please go," David said a little quieter, genuine concern coloring his voice. "You would not want anything unpleasant to happen to Mrs. Patton."

Lucinda sighed and unfolded her arms. "I suppose Mrs. Patton and I should go to the lace shop before it closes for the day."

"Thank you," he said.

Lucinda nodded as she pulled on her gloves. "Make sure you show the constable the disparity between Baxter's numbers and the rest of the clerks' ledgers. And I don't think Quill and Baxter were working together. Baxter would not have risked his own payout for such a small sum as Quill skimmed. His ledger should be considered separately."

"I do believe that you are correct," David said. "And both will have to answer to the law and to our investors for the missing funds."

David folded the paper on the desk and placed it in his coat pocket. Lucinda tied the bow of her bonnet crookedly and said, "Your next interviews will not be pleasant."

"I should think not," David said.

Unpleasant did not begin to describe David's afternoon. Mr. Baxter's denials and begging for clemency for the sake of his family left David with a sick feeling in his stomach. Mr. Quill, who David learned was in fact the pimply fellow, happened to be the sole support for an indigent mother and three sisters. He had stolen the money to pay for his mother's expensive medicines and unpaid doctor's bills.

In the end, David decided not to press legal charges against either gentleman. He politely dismissed the constable and came to an agreement with Mr. Baxter. Baxter promised to repay the entire sum to the company within a fortnight, and he would find new employment elsewhere. David could not allow such a man to hold a position of trust in the company again, and he couldn't give him a reference. But he chose not to ruin him either.

Mr. Quill was a young man like David, and the amount he stole was a pittance in comparison. And even though Quill's actions were wrong, his motives were noble. So David gave him a twenty-pound note to pay off his family's remaining doctor's debts and a second chance to keep his position. Mr. Quill sobbed as he accepted both. He tearfully promised that he would never steal again, and David believed him.

David looked at his pocket watch. He would barely have time enough to arrive at the hotel, freshen up, and change his clothes for dinner.

When he arrived at his room, his dinner coat was laid out and a fresh pitcher of water and a basin stood ready on the bureau. He poured the water over his hands and scrubbed each finger with the provided bar of soap. It felt good to wash off the grime from the day. He ran his wet fingers through his hair, splashed his face with water from the basin, and then dried off with the towel.

David did not dawdle as he changed his raiment, and yet when he entered the hotel's supper room, he saw Mrs. Patton and Lucinda already waiting for him. Lucinda looked as if she had spent an entire day getting ready for dinner. Each of her dark curls was perfectly placed in a halo around her face. She wore an opal pendant on a ribbon, which drew his attention to her shapely neck. The scarlet of her gown brought out the auburn highlights in her nearly black hair.

Lucinda walked toward him and tucked her arm in his. "Admiring me, David?" she whispered.

He turned his head toward hers, only inches away. "I was debating which was more fetching, you or your dress."

She angled her head to the side. "And?"

"Definitely the dress."

Lucinda laughed and gave him another dazzling smile. They sat at the table, and the waiter quickly brought the first course: brussels sprouts glazed in a white sauce.

"Shall I give this dress to you as a gift?" Lucinda asked in an undertone so only David could hear.

"I don't think it will have quite the same allure without you in it."

Lucinda nodded. "Besides, I don't think it would fit you at all. You're rather too thick around the middle."

David laughed loudly in surprise, and Mrs. Patton asked primly what the pair had found to be so diverting.

"The brussels sprouts," Lucinda said. "Mr. Randall was hoping to get the recipe for his mother's cook. Is that not so?"

"Precisely."

Mrs. Patton looked from David to Lucinda and then said, "Quite a compliment to their cook, I daresay. I hope the next course is a little more sustaining."

The next five courses were perfectly adequate, and Mrs. Patton attempted to keep appropriate conversation at the table. The hot weather was discussed at great length, followed by the equally dull subject of trains and how frequently they stopped. David was relieved when the plates were cleared from the table. For the last two courses, all he could think of was his well-aired room and soft pillow. But he should have known that Lucinda would have more plans.

"You cannot retire yet," she protested. "You have to escort Mrs. Patton and myself to a concert at the Assembly Rooms."

David almost opened his mouth to refuse, but he saw the stubborn turn of her chin and realized that in the end he would most likely give in to her anyway. He always had when they were children. "Shall I call for a carriage?"

"It's only a short walk," Lucinda assured him and Mrs. Patton.

David had a lady on each arm as they walked down the cobblestone street on the way to the Assembly Rooms. Lucinda insisted they first stop at the Pump Room for a glass of the famous waters. David took one sip of the tepid water before returning his glass to the attendant. He would have happily paid twice as much not to drink that distasteful water again. Mrs. Patton drained her glass easily, and Lucinda choked down nearly half of hers before declaring, "I can't drink any more of it."

They moved from the Pump Room to the Assembly Rooms, where he purchased their tickets and assisted them to their seats near the rear of the music room. The concert began shortly after their arrival. The tenor had a massive belly and a round face and sang several songs in Italian. David glanced at Lucinda; she was primly watching the concert with her gloved hands folded in her lap. Beside her, Mrs. Patton had, as usual, fallen asleep while sitting up.

Lucinda caught his eye and gave him a wink.

"It appears your chaperone has fallen asleep again," he whispered in her ear. "It's a pity she couldn't have at dinner."

"I should have told you, David," Lucinda whispered back, "Mrs. Patton never falls asleep when there is food present."

David laughed and pretended to cough. "Are you enjoying the concert?"

"Very much," Lucinda said. "But I have no idea what is being sung. The music is very pretty, though. Do you speak Italian?"

"A little bit," David said modestly.

Lucinda arched one eyebrow and gave him a doubting look.

"I read Latin fluently and Italian is not all that different," he said. "I understand more than I can speak."

"Pray tell me, what is this song about?"

"A fickle woman," he said.

Lucinda scowled at him and whispered, "Stop teasing me this instant."

David feigned innocence. "'*La donna è mobile*—the woman is flighty.'"

"And?"

"'Like a feather in the wind, she changes in voice and in thought. Always miserable is he who trusts her. He who confides in her his unwary heart!'"

Lucinda wrinkled her nose and pursed her lips. "I think I preferred the music before I knew what he was singing about."

She did not speak for several more songs, but then added, "It is ridiculous to assume that women are more inconsistent than men."

"What of your story?" David countered. "Isn't Eurydice Emerson fickle? Why can she not pick one of her suitors instead of keeping both men waiting on her whims?"

"You've read it, then!" Lucinda said a little too loudly.

Several people looked back at them. David could see her color heighten, but thought her blush made her even more becoming.

Once all eyes were again on the singer, Lucinda leaned closer to David and whispered, "Eurydice is not a fickle character. She just hasn't made up her mind yet. There are qualities in both suitors that she admires. She needed a little more time to know her heart, and alas, the author, Mrs. Smith, died before she could give Eurydice that time."

David considered this. "If she required time to select a suitor, she was not in love with either of them," he whispered back.

Lucinda smiled. "Why, David, I would never have guessed you to be a romantic."

David flushed at these words, seeming to heat up underneath the intensity of her gaze, the nearness of her body to his. This discussion had become too personal. "Besides, Mr. Thisbe is an annoying chap," he added in a light tone. "He has no faults at all and is too inclined to give sermons. She should have married Lord Dunstan and been done with it already."

"But what of Lord Dunstan's mysterious past?" Lucinda asked. "Mrs. Smith died before Lord Dunstan could confess to Eurydice what he did. He could have done something quite dreadful, you know."

"Nothing he did could be as dreadful as having to live with someone who gives sermons on a daily basis."

Lucinda choked in an attempt not to laugh. David found the sound entirely charming. He turned in his seat to see Lucinda's face, instead of just her profile. He felt the large hoop of her skirt brush his leg as she turned toward him as well. She opened her mouth to speak when the music stopped and the room filled with the sound of applause.

"Is the concert over already?" Mrs. Patton asked.

Six

LUCINDA FELT A BUBBLE OF anticipation in her stomach. She was possibly going to discover the identity of the author Mrs. Smith, and finally learn how the story was supposed to end. She dressed with care that morning, stepping into her crinoline cage—a steel-framed petticoat that made her skirts look perfectly rounded—and tying the strings at her waist. Then she put on a blue dress with a pattern of little yellow flowers. She pinched her cheeks and smiled at her reflection. Blue was a very good color on her.

Mrs. Patton ate breakfast as if she had never eaten another meal in her life. Lucinda wondered again how such a small woman could eat so very much. David also had an appetite that was astonishing. He ate three sausages, four pieces of bacon, three eggs, and three slices of toast. When they were finished, a full-bosomed young maid giggled at David as she removed their dirty plates. He gave her a slight smile in return, and Lucinda felt an unaccountable urge to first pour her cup of tea down the front of the girl's dress and then empty the rest of the teapot onto David's head.

After breakfast, Lucinda and Mrs. Patton returned to their rooms to finish packing their trunks. Once she had closed the latch on her trunk and locked it, Lucinda put on her straw bonnet and tied the blue ribbon to the side of her chin. She left the trunk—they would ask a servant to bring the luggage down—and descended the stairs to the main sitting room, where David was waiting with his portmanteau. As she approached, he took her hand and bowed over it.

"You look very pretty this morning, Lucinda."

Mrs. Patton arrived just in time to spoil the moment. "Mr. Randall," she said, "would you please have a servant fetch our trunks?"

David released Lucinda's hand and then briefly bent over Mrs. Patton's before leaving the room.

Mrs. Patton gave a long sigh and said wistfully, "How nice it will be to be back home. I never sleep as well away from my own bed."

David returned a quarter of an hour later and escorted both ladies to a hired carriage, where their trunks were already tied onto the rear. Lucinda sat with her back to the driver and

Mrs. Patton sat beside her with a long sigh. David directed the driver to number fifteen Laura Place, and then sat on the seat facing forward.

"Thank you, Miss Leavitt," David said, acknowledging her thoughtfulness.

"I am only protecting my favorite dress," Lucinda explained. "I do not wish for you to be sick on it."

"Lucinda!" Mrs. Patton chided. "Ladies do not speak of such things *ever*."

Lucinda shrugged and looked out her window. She could see the River Avon flowing fast as they approached the most interesting bridge she had ever seen. There were shops built from limestone on both sides of the bridge, elegant buildings with arched entries and Doric pilasters. Laura Place was situated at the end of Pulteney Bridge.

The carriage pulled up in front of number fifteen. David opened the door and stepped out, then turned back to hand out the ladies.

"Are we not going to the train station?" Mrs. Patton asked as she descended.

"Mr. Randall has a small piece of business to conduct here first," Lucinda said.

"A little matter of business between Emerson, Dunstan, and Thisbe," David said, looking pleased when Lucinda laughed.

He held her elbow as they climbed the stairs. David tapped on the door four times with his cane. A servant answered and asked what their business was.

David handed the servant his card. "I should like to speak to your proprietor on an important matter."

The servant looked at the expensive gilt-edged card and then ushered them into a small, stuffy sitting room decorated in shades of rose pink. "I shall tell the mistress you are here."

The servant left the room, and Mrs. Patton immediately sat on the closest chair. Lucinda chose a seat next to David on the sofa. The servant returned quickly, followed by a plump woman with a turned-up nose and droopy cheeks that reminded Lucinda of a pug dog.

"How may I 'elp you?" she asked civilly.

"Are you the proprietor of this establishment?" David asked.

"I am Mrs. Wilson and own this 'ouse," she said with pride.

"I understand that you let rooms," Lucinda said. "I was wondering if, by chance, you have a registry of your guests with their forwarding addresses? I am—we are—trying to locate a Mrs. Smith. As I said in the letter I wrote to you last week inquiring after her."

"I may 'ave received a letter," Mrs. Wilson said, stroking her jowls. "And what business is it of yours?"

Lucinda's mouth hung open in surprise. She was about to tell the woman exactly what she thought of her, when David touched her arm lightly. She closed her mouth and clenched her teeth.

"We are attempting to locate Mrs. Smith's final papers," David answered smoothly. "We know it is a great inconvenience to you, and we are happy to compensate you for your precious time."

"What sort of compensation?"

David handed the woman a couple of crowns. She showed her teeth and her droopy cheeks wiggled.

"One moment, good sir," Mrs. Wilson said and left the room. She returned with a registry book of all her visitors and handed it to David. He immediately passed the book on to Lucinda, who eagerly turned the pages. Her enthusiasm wore off as she waded through countless lines of Leatherbys, Joneses, Clarks, and Porters. Lucinda chewed on her thumbnail as she continued to turn the pages. And then at last she saw it—Mr. and Mrs. Smith, stayed from January to March.

"Might I have a pen and paper?" Lucinda asked.

Mrs. Wilson looked from Lucinda to David. He reached into his pocket and took out a silver coin between his fingers. Mrs. Wilson deftly snatched the coin, and when she smiled, it was a frightening thing; she was missing several teeth and the rest were yellow.

"Happy to oblige the quality," she said with another ingratiating smile. "I'll have my servant nip out and fetch you a pen and a paper."

Mrs. Wilson snapped her fingers. The servant bolted from the room and returned quite quickly with a small stack of paper, an ink bottle, and a pen, and held them out to David. Lucinda clucked her tongue in annoyance. David gave her a sympathetic look as he handed her the writing supplies. She took the lid off the ink bottle, dipped the pen inside and copied down:

Mr. and Mrs. Smith, Shaftesbury

Lucinda read the next few lines, which consisted of six different payments, but no further explanation of their direction. She copied everything down anyway, then set aside the pen and bit her thumbnail. It wasn't much at all, but at least they had another clue.

"I think that's all," she said. "There's nothing else of importance here."

She closed the book and was about to hand it back to the servant when David said, "No."

"No?" Lucinda asked in surprise.

David flipped the book back open. "We ought to write down the names and directions of every guest that stayed here during January through the first week of March, when Mrs. Smith died. We don't know the name of the person who wrote to Mr. Gibbs. Perhaps we can track them down by sending out further inquiries."

Lucinda blinked at him. "That is a very sound idea, David," she said. "Why don't you read them out to me, and I will write them down."

David slowly and meticulously read out every single person who had stayed at number fifteen Laura Place during that time. Lucinda wrote down all of their names and addresses until her hand began to cramp.

"How many more?" she asked, setting down the pen so she could shake out her hand.

"Only one," David said, pointing to a name in the book. "A Mrs. Burntwood and her personal companion. Burntwood Folly near Reading."

Lucinda diligently added Mrs. Burntwood to the bottom of the third page. She set down the pen again and blew on the paper until the ink dried. She placed the first two pages on top of it, and David returned the book to Mrs. Wilson with a bow. Her jowls turned a fiery red as she thanked him.

Mrs. Patton was snoring in her seat. Lucinda stood and gently shook her shoulder. "Time to go, Mrs. Patton."

She sat up straight and blinked rapidly.

"I am ready," she declared. Lucinda put a hand underneath Mrs. Patton's elbow to help her up, but the older woman shook her off. "I am not so old yet as to need assistance."

"Of course, not," David agreed, and opened the door for both ladies.

The trip to the train station was uneventful, and they were boarded and settled into their own compartment with remarkable ease.

Mrs. Patton sat contentedly beside Lucinda, and within a quarter of an hour fell asleep. Lucinda looked at David, who had taken off his beaver hat and was using it to fan himself.

"It is so hot and stuffy in here," Lucinda said.

"Unbearably so," David agreed.

"I'm going to open the window." Lucinda tried to slide open the small window, but she had no luck.

"Shall I?"

Lucinda didn't respond to David's offer. Instead, she stood up and gave the handle a great yank. The window slid open much faster than she was expecting; she lost her balance and with an undignified yelp fell backward onto David's lap.

As he put his hands around her waist to steady her, Lucinda found herself breathless and blushing. She stood again just as the train came to a stop, and she fell back into his lap. She could feel his breath on her ear and his soft laughter.

"May I assist you now?" he asked.

Without waiting for her reply, David lifted her from his lap and onto the seat beside him. Their shoulders still touched. Her large skirt still brushed against his pant legs. Lucinda felt breathless again. She was grateful for the small breeze of air on her hot cheeks coming from the newly opened window.

"See? It isn't too difficult to accept assistance every now and again," David said in his cockiest manner.

"I have accepted your help with my search for the author."

David chuckled. "I don't think you accepted my assistance so much as demanded it."

Lucinda laughed, and then they were laughing together. She felt again the warm camaraderie that they once had shared in their youth.

David was silent for several moments before he asked, "I am curious why finding Mrs. Smith is so important to you. It is only a story, after all."

"I suppose if it was only a story, I am being very silly."

"I was not saying that."

"Mrs. Smith was more to me than just a story," Lucinda explained. "I found Mrs. Smith's books about a year after I started finishing school."

"And?"

Lucinda smiled wryly. "I had no friends at school. No acquaintances. For none of the girls wished to be associated with a girl of low birth, who even the teachers despised. And then I discovered Mrs. Smith's serialized story, *East and West*, and her fictional characters became my only companions. And when that book was finished, the magazine began to publish her next story—*She Knew She Was Right*. Eurydice Emerson is the closest thing I have to a friend."

David was silent for several more moments. "I am your friend," he said. "And we will just have to find out if your Mrs. Smith left any clues for us. Where was the woman from again?"

"Shaftesbury."

"I know that town," David said. "I've passed through it many times. It's not more than five miles from my cousin Alfred's estate."

"I would suggest we set out at once," Lucinda said, "but I know you have a great deal of business to attend to."

David nodded.

The train began to move forward again. Lucinda leaned her head back against the seat and looked out the window. They sat in what Lucinda thought was companionable silence, until she realized that David had fallen asleep. Lucinda smiled to herself. Then the train gave a small lurch, and David's head fell onto her shoulder and rested there.

Lucinda's heartbeat quickened. She held her breath, but David didn't wake up. He rubbed his cheek into the fabric of her sleeve and then rested contentedly. Lucinda looked across the compartment at Mrs. Patton. She too was still sleeping soundly.

Lucinda exhaled slowly. She felt uncomfortable with his proximity, but also thrilled at his closeness to her. Not just because he was an attractive gentleman, which he undoubtedly was. But because no one had really touched her since her mother died.

Her mother. That tall, beautiful, black-haired woman who had held Lucinda in her arms and sang her to sleep. Who had danced with Lucinda and sang "Ring Around the Rosie." Who had wiped away Lucinda's tears and plaited her hair. Lucinda remembered the last time she had touched her mother—it was while she lay in her coffin. Her mother's skin had felt cold and her face did not look quite right. Lucinda's last memory of her mother was kissing her cheek, with her father standing by her side, weeping.

After her mother's death, her father never embraced her,

but simply patted her on the head if she did something that pleased him. The servants kept a respectful distance from her, and as she had admitted to David, she had no real friends. The only contact she had with others was through gloves while dancing. And there was definitely a thrill to have a man's hand on her waist, but this feeling was different. More wholesome. Warm.

Maybe I do have a real friend after all.

She wanted to touch another person with her hands. To feel her skin upon the skin of another. *But would it be an intrusion?* Lucinda wondered, then reconciled her conscience that if anyone was intruding, it was he by laying his head on her shoulder. She waved aside the thought that he was sleeping and he hadn't purposely done it. She exhaled slowly again and pulled off one of her gloves. She gently placed her fingers in his hair and softly ran them through it. David opened his eyes slowly and blinked. Lucinda watched his face as he realized where he was and what he was doing. He sat up quickly, nearly bumping the side of his head into her face.

"I am so sorry, Miss Lea—Lucinda," he said without his usual poise, a red blotch suffusing his neck. "I did not realize that I had—that I was—forgive me."

Lucinda shrugged slightly. "I do not mind. I am used to my companions falling asleep."

He grinned at her and she returned it. Lucinda looked down at her gloveless hand. The glove was no longer in her lap, but on the floor of the compartment. Before she could stoop down to reach it, David had picked it up. It was Lucinda's turn to blush. He handed her the glove and gazed at her questioningly, with one eyebrow raised.

"I—I—I was just fixing your hair."

"My hair?"

"Yes," Lucinda lied. "It was quite mussed up and I was trying to make you look respectable."

"And how is my hair now?" David asked.

His usually meticulously combed hair was, in fact, a disaster. If anything, when Lucinda had touched it she'd made it messier than before.

"Picturesque."

David laughed and attempted to pat his hair down. Lucinda's ungloved hand, seemingly of its own volition, reached over and carefully smoothed down his curls.

"You're presentable now."

"My many thanks," he said.

Mrs. Patton snorted. David and Lucinda jolted farther apart on their side of the compartment, David crushing his beaver top hat as he sat upon it. Mrs. Patton blinked as he pulled his top hat out from underneath him.

"Lucinda, why are you sitting over there without me?"

Lucinda peeked at David, who was busying himself with pushing out the top of his smashed hat. It was very crumpled and would never be the same.

"I was just hot," Lucinda managed. "I could feel the breeze from the window better from this side. But I am quite cool now and will return by you."

Lucinda felt anything but cool, but she stood anyway and

returned to the seat next to her chaperone. Mrs. Patton let out a long sigh and said cheerfully, "I do so enjoy a good train ride."

"As do I," David said soulfully. "As do I."

Lucinda bit her lip to keep from laughing.

Seven

"I HAVE SENT MR. MURPHY," DAVID explained to Mr. Leavitt. "He shall take over the Bath office until a suitable replacement is found for Mr. Baxter."

"Excellent choice," Mr. Leavitt said. "There is not another fellow in the company that I trust more than he. And of course, you, Randall. I am impressed you discovered the pigeon-livered fopdoodle. I shudder to think what that fellow could have done left unchecked."

"Some of the credit should go to your daughter," David told him.

Mr. Leavitt leaned forward in his chair. "Lucy? Lucy has nothing to do with the business these days! She was only in Bath to purchase lace."

David realized in that moment that Lucinda had learned at least one thing at finishing school—the art of lying. The girl he'd known had no guile, but the woman it seemed was positively made of it. "Oh . . . it . . . it was just something Miss Leavitt said that made me look closer into the Bath office."

Mr. Leavitt seemed to accept the explanation, because he sat back in his tall wingback chair. He gestured to all the piles of paper on his desk. "We are burdened with too much business at the moment."

"The best kind of burden."

"Yes," Mr. Leavitt agreed. "But I have been thinking of late that we might need to bring another man on. Someone to handle the internal finances, oversee the ledgers and such. Chief financial officer for the company. Prevent a Bath situation from reoccurring."

"Do you have someone in mind, Mr. Leavitt?"

"Presently, no," Mr. Leavitt said. "But I thought you might keep an eye out for such a man. You're young and you move so much more in society than I am inclined to."

"I will."

David left his partner's office and returned to his own down the hall. His desk was equally laden with unfinished tasks that kept him there late almost every night. Part of David wanted to ask one of the clerks for assistance, but he couldn't. It would be like admitting that his father was right. That David couldn't handle the workload. That he wasn't clever enough for the business.

He ran his fingers through his hair, which reminded him of Lucinda and waking up next to her on the train. Why had she lied to him? He knew she wanted to travel to Bath to find out about the author, but why did she lie about the audit? Not that David rated Mrs. Patton's intelligence very highly, but Mr. Leavitt was no fool.

Lucinda plagued his thoughts for the rest of his workday. He accomplished less than he should have, which meant he would have all the more to do tomorrow, but he'd promised his mother that he'd escort her to the Butterfields' party that night.

His mother was waiting for him when he arrived home. He gave her a kiss on the cheek and promised not to be more than a quarter of an hour changing into his dinner clothes. David's valet was ready and waiting to assist him in dressing.

Once finished, David stepped quickly down the stairs, and his mother stood to meet him. She was a small woman with dark hair and large brown eyes surrounded by several wrinkles. She smiled at him. "You're late, son," she said playfully.

"I am a disgrace," David agreed, and led her out to the carriage.

He sat next to his mother and tapped his cane to the top of the carriage to signal the driver to go.

"You're as handsome as your father," his mother said fondly. "If only you could find a nice young lady to marry."

David stiffened at the comparison to his father. "I am in no hurry to marry, Mother. I'm barely nineteen years of age."

"I know," his mother agreed with a wistful sigh. "I married your father when I was nineteen."

"I am much too busy with business right now."

"I hope you are not too busy that you have forgotten your aunt's invitation to stay at Keynsham Hall next week."

David groaned. He had forgotten it entirely. "Could you possibly attend without me?"

His mother shook her head. "I could not. You promised me you would attend, and if you do not, your aunt's numbers will be off. There will not be enough gentlemen, and you know how infrequently she can entertain these days because of their straitened circumstances. And how much work she puts into planning her house parties."

"Very well," David said. "I will bring my work with me."

David knew his mother well enough to read the expression on her face. She wasn't pleased with this response, but was willing to leave the argument for another time. His mother was all smiles as he escorted her into the Butterfields' home and greeted the hosts. David nodded civilly to his many acquaintances. He left his mother talking to her friend Lady Swithen and was slowly making his way to the cardroom. He was in no mood to dance and make inane conversation with debutantes this evening.

He passed through the dancing room and stopped midstep when he saw Lucinda. Indeed she was impossible to miss. She was nearly a head taller than any lady present and even some of the gentlemen. Her dark curls seemed to shine in the light of the gas lamps, and her blue eyes sparkled like the stones at her throat. She was dancing with some fellow a few inches shorter than her. When Lucinda caught his gaze on her, she winked at him, and continued to dance with her partner.

"Your Miss Leavitt is a goddess," a voice said in his ear. "Aphrodite."

David recalled his surroundings. "Alfred, how are you this evening?"

"Better now, my dear cousin David," he said. "Definitely better."

David crushed down a feeling of irritation. "It seems an agreeable party."

Alfred gave a catlike smile. "An agreeable party needs only beautiful ladies, of which I see plenty."

"I shall leave you to them, Cousin," David said with a curt nod.

He continued to the cardroom and played several hands of whist and a couple rounds of piquet. But his mind was not on cards, and he lost nearly fifty guineas. Mr. Winter suggested another hand, but David respectfully declined. Instead, he stood and found himself walking back to the dancing room, where he found Lucinda dancing with Alfred. He saw her laugh, and his feeling of irritation changed to a darker one of anger. David turned to leave the room, when for the second time that evening someone was standing at his elbow.

Miss Clara Hardin placed her gloved hand on his arm. "Excuse me, Mr. Randall. I did not see you there."

When Miss Hardin did not release her hold on his arm, David mechanically asked her if she would like to dance. She accepted, and he led her to join the set.

Dancing with Miss Hardin wasn't too great a sacrifice, David admitted to himself. She was a pretty young lady with blond curls, dark blue eyes, and a rosebud of a mouth set in a permanent pout. David went through the motions of the dance, but his mind was still on Lucinda. Miss Hardin supplied conversation about the hotness of the weather and the latest gossip about another possible wedding in the royal family. David only nodded in response until finally the musicians played their concluding notes, and he led Miss Hardin to the side of the room.

David told himself it was only coincidence that he was leading them near to where Lucinda and Alfred were standing.

"You and your chaperone must join my mother's house party next week," he overheard Alfred say.

"I am not sure if we can," Lucinda demurred.

"I shan't take no for an answer," Alfred said, eyeing David and Miss Hardin. "Ah, Miss Leavitt, allow me to introduce you to another lady who will be one of our party, Miss Hardin."

"But we are already acquainted, Lord Adlington," Miss Hardin said, and gave Lucinda a cold nod.

Lucinda returned an even colder one, her pert nose slightly turned up. "We attended finishing school together."

"And my cousin David you already know," Alfred said.

"Good evening, Mr. Randall," Lucinda said, and curtsied to him.

David bowed.

"Miss Leavitt was just telling me that she will not dance with me a third time," Alfred said and held out his hand to David's partner. "Miss Hardin, would you take pity on a poor fellow and dance with me?"

"Yes, Lord Adlington," she said in her breathy voice. "It would be my honor."

Miss Hardin released her hold on David's hand and took his cousin's. Alfred gave David a nod as he led Miss Hardin back to the dance floor. David stood next to Lucinda but said nothing.

"You are supposed to ask me to dance with you," Lucinda supplied.

"I don't feel like dancing."

"I would be delighted to accept," Lucinda said, and before he knew it, her hand was in his.

They walked a few steps before he put a hand on her waist and gently led her through the first turn. She responded instinctively to his lead. He felt her warmth through his gloves and resolutely looked away from her, trying to focus on something else.

Anything else.

"Don't be such a spoilsport, David," Lucinda whispered. "You looked at me the entire time I danced with your cousin, and now that I am dancing with you, you won't look at me at all."

David found her smiling face so close to his own. Her height made the distance between them seem insignificant. He could feel her warm breath on his cheek and could smell the scent of flowers on her body. Thinking was difficult; speaking seemed impossible. In his chest was a confusing mixture of anger and attraction. He wanted to wipe the smile off her mocking lips, but he also felt an overwhelming urge to kiss those same lips.

"You just trod on my toes."

"No, I did not," Lucinda said, but glanced down at their feet. She looked back up to his face and laughed. "But don't worry, I plan to trod on your toes very soon."

"And yet, I stand here unafraid."

"Oh, David, you should be. You. Should. Be. Afraid."

Before David could respond, the music ended and all the couples clapped. He led Lucinda to the side of the ballroom and bowed over her gloved hand.

"Thank you for asking me to dance, *Mr.* Randall," Lucinda said with another of her infernal winks. "I am very tired and very thirsty."

David did not reply, but he didn't walk away either.

"Now you are supposed to offer to fetch me a glass of punch and find me a chair," Lucinda whispered dramatically. "They covered this very clearly in finishing school."

"I do not wish to do that either," he said at last.

"What have I done to make you so uncivil?" she asked with her eyebrows raised.

A dozen retorts sprung to David's mind—none of which were appropriate in present circumstances—so he took Lucinda's elbow and led her to the refreshment table, where he procured her a glass of punch and handed it to her. He accepted a second glass for himself and then led her to a sofa. He sat beside her as she sipped her punch daintily.

"I see you are acquainted with the Butterfields," he managed at last.

"Yes, Miss Butterfield attended Miss Holley's Finishing School," Lucinda said.

"I thought you had no friends at school."

"Friend is probably not the most correct term for our relationship," Lucinda explained. "Miss Butterfield is of a religious inclination and wishes to become a foreign missionary. She feels it imperative to socialize with those of lower classes to acclimatize herself to their uncivilized ways."

David was drinking as she said this and choked on his punch. Lucinda lifted her glass to her mouth and sipped as if nothing had happened.

"I spoke to your father today," David said at last.

"Ah," Lucinda said. She tapped the side of her nose twice with her index finger. "I see why you are upset with me."

"He had no idea that you had helped with the ledgers. Nor that you had audited the Bath office with me."

"You make it sound so scandalous," Lucinda replied. "Mrs. Patton was present the entire time."

"Sleeping."

"*Presently* sleeping."

Then suddenly the question was out of him before he knew he had spoken it. "Why did you lie to me? I thought we were friends again."

Lucinda swallowed. "Because I thought you would not allow me to help with the business if you knew the truth."

"Well, now you will never know, because you did not trust me."

"I trusted you once, and you know the result of that."

"Do not try to put me in the wrong this time," David said. "You lied to me. You used me. And you—"

"You . . . ?" Lucinda prompted.

"You—Mother, may I introduce you to Miss Leavitt?" David said, standing.

"Miss Leavitt, how you have grown," she said. "You look very much like your mother."

"Thank you, ma'am," Lucinda said as she stood. "Please, take my seat on the sofa. Your son was so kind as to let me rest this dance."

His mother took her up on the offer. "Well, it appears, Miss Leavitt, that you owe my son a dance."

"Surely you do not wish for us to abandon you just as you arrive, Mother."

"Nonsense," she said. "Young people should be dancing."

David reluctantly held out his hand to Lucinda, and she placed her gloved hand in his. The memory of her ungloved hand fixing his hair flashed into his mind. He glanced over to her and wondered if she was remembering the same thing. He led her to the dance floor and then put his hand on her waist. *It would be another waltz,* he thought dourly. He did not want to be this close to her. He did not want to touch her. And he certainly did not want to smell the fragrance of flowers that always seemed to cling to her body.

"I am sorry that I misled you," Lucinda said quietly, leaning closer to him. David felt his senses heighten at her nearness. "I should have told you the truth, but if you will allow me, I will tell you now."

David made the mistake of looking into her depthless blue eyes. He could see a myriad of emotions reflected in there: contrition, defiance, and another he could not identify. He turned his gaze away, but nodded slightly. He felt Lucinda lean in still farther—the space between them was nearly nonexistent.

"I hoped when I returned from school, having dutifully learned how to act like a lady, I would be allowed to come back to the business," Lucinda said. "But my father would not hear of it. He said I did not belong in the countinghouse. He engaged Mrs. Patton to chaperone me and assist my entrance into higher society. The society where he is not welcome nor wanted. And I tried to please him. I tried to interest myself in the busy nothings of a woman of means, but there is no alleviation to the boredom. The endless waiting to receive calls or to go visiting. And the household finances take me less than an hour a fortnight to complete. David, my mind was made for more than this. I am capable of so much more than this. Can you not understand?"

David deftly led her around another dancing couple. "What I don't understand is why you lied to me."

"I thought you would defer to my father's wishes. To society's rigid protocols that would have me leave my mind to waste because I was not born a man."

"I do not know what I would have done. But I would have preferred you to be honest with me."

"Were two days in my company so very intolerable?" Lucinda asked.

David felt the corners of his lips go up in a reluctant smile. "Wretched."

Lucinda laughed at this. "You are unkind. I was on my best behavior!"

"If that was your best behavior, I shudder to think of what is in store for me in the future."

"Then you are not cutting my acquaintance entirely?" she asked in a tight voice, her eyes downcast.

The music stopped, but David stayed on the dance floor. He put his hand underneath her chin and lifted her face up so that he looked directly into her eyes. "I dare not cut it entirely."

"Because of my father."

"No, Lucinda," he said, releasing his hold on her chin, "because then I would never discover the fate of the impecunious Eurydice Emerson."

Lucinda smiled. "That would be tragic."

"Unthinkable."

And they laughed together as friends.

David looked at the grandfather clock in his office. It was already past six in the evening. He had only three days until his aunt's house party and a mountain of papers sat on his desk. He could not possibly finish them all in time before his trip to his cousin's estate in Dorset.

His mind returned again to Lucinda, but he wished it wouldn't. He wasn't sure if he'd entirely forgiven her for her deception. Still, it seemed ironic that he had more work to do than one person could possibly accomplish, and she had no work at all to do and complained of being bored at home.

A thought occurred to David as he picked up several papers to bring home with him: Why not ask Lucinda for her help? Her father had specifically asked her not to come to the countinghouse, but nothing had been said about working at home. He looked at the papers he was already bringing home, then separated them into two piles. One pile consisted of business that he needed to complete himself and the other pile consisted of papers and analyses of financial numbers.

David picked up more papers from his desk and continued to divide the workload between himself and Lucinda until every item on his desk had been accounted for. He picked up his leather bag and carefully placed all the documents for

Lucinda inside of it, then put on his coat and hat. He grabbed his cane with one hand and his leather bag with the other and left his office. A quick glance down the hall showed him the gas lamp in Mr. Leavitt's office was still burning.

David locked the door to the building behind him and hailed a hansom cab, directing the driver to the Leavitts' home. When they arrived, he alighted from the cab and dashed up the front steps, knocking on the Leavitts' door with his cane. The butler opened the door. He recognized David and immediately let him inside and led him to the front sitting room.

"I will let Miss Leavitt know you are here," the butler said with a bow, and left the room.

David had not waited long when the butler opened the door to the room for Lucinda. He stood as she entered. She was wearing a dark purple evening gown, and a necklace of amethysts adorned her throat. She dismissed the butler, who closed the door behind him.

Lucinda walked toward David and stopped a yard shy of him. She idly played with a shepherdess figurine on the table beside her. "What odd hours you choose to make social calls, David. Morning calls are supposed to be made between the hours of three and five, before dinner. We've already eaten dinner and Mrs. Patton is finishing her toilette, and then we are off to an engagement at the Calders'. Shall I see you there?"

David shook his head. "I am afraid that I have a great deal of business to attend to."

Lucinda nodded at this. "Would you like to sit down?"

"I do not intend to take that much of your time, Lucinda," David said.

He placed his leather bag on the table next to the shepherdess figurine, opened it, and pulled out the stack of papers.

"What are these for?"

"You," he said simply. "I have too much to do and you too little. I thought you might be willing to assist me with these, for a regular salary, of course."

David had barely finished speaking when Lucinda threw her arms around his neck and embraced him tightly. He inhaled her intoxicating scent and enjoyed the pleasure of her soft body pressed against his. She looked up into his face. He could see her usually creamy neck was red. She released her hold on him and stepped back.

"I hope my embrace was not too wretched for you to endure," she said. "I am just so delighted. Thank you so much for including me in the business."

"Not too wretched," David assured her, and then attempted to collect his wits and senses by focusing back on the business at hand. "If you will give me a few moments to explain what I need accomplished, I will be on my way and you can go to your party."

Eight

LUCINDA SAT ON THE EDGE of her seat in the carriage. Traveling was not nearly as enjoyable without David, though she felt warm inside just thinking about him. David had brought her work to do. *Real* work. Important business papers, and he had treated her as an equal, not as a member of the "weaker sex" who needed to be protected and pampered.

Besides the two days in Bath spent in David's company, Lucinda could not think of a time she'd enjoyed herself more than completing the assignments he had given her. The numbers seemed to speak to her, to dance in her mind in perfect harmony. She loved comparing offers and debating the return on investment versus the cost of production and the profit margin. Numbers were so neat and tidy. So exact. Feelings and people were much messier. It was harder to know the right answer and how everything would equal out in the end.

As the carriage pulled into the gravel driveway of Keynsham Hall, Lucinda could not resist poking her head out the window for a better look. It was just the sort of estate the mysterious Lord Dunstan would have owned. The main part of the building looked as if it were several centuries old—like a medieval cathedral with large arched windows and porticos. To the south stood a wing of the house that resembled Tudor architecture with its narrow windows and U shape. The north wing looked to be the newest addition to the house; probably less than a hundred years old, in the Georgian style. It was perfectly perpendicular with three rows of evenly spaced windows.

The park itself was equally eye-catching. The house stood on a slight hill surrounded on the south by a large lake and the north by a thick, densely forested area. Lucinda could see a couple of overgrown formal gardens in the center with a large fountain on each side of the driveway. She leaned her head farther out the window to get a better view.

"Lucinda, sit back in your seat this instant," Mrs. Patton said sharply. "What will the Adlingtons think if they see you gawking like a commoner?"

Lucinda bit down her retort that she *was* in fact a commoner and reluctantly obeyed. Truthfully, she had only accepted Lord Adlington's invitation to Keynsham Hall because of its close proximity to the village of Shaftesbury. Lucinda was playing her cards close. She wanted her father and Mrs. Patton to believe that she was a willing debutante, eager to be invited to society parties. But in reality, she was only there to inquire after Mrs. Smith's surviving family. So she continued to look out the window of the carriage, but most of the view was obscured by the angle of the window. When they finally came to stop, a liveried servant opened the door and assisted Mrs. Patton and Lucinda out.

Lord Adlington stood only a few feet away. He was not quite as tall nor as handsome as his cousin David; Alfred's chin was round and his face a little too fleshy, but he had nice brown eyes and a dashing mustache. He strode toward them with a welcoming smile, his hand outstretched. He leaned over Mrs. Patton's hand with great ceremony and then Lucinda's. He grinned at her as he released his hold on her hand.

"Allow me to introduce you to my mother, Lady Mary Adlington," he said.

Lady Mary gave a perfectly executed curtsy. She had the same round chin as her son and the hint of a second one. She smiled, but unlike her son it did not reach her eyes and she didn't speak a word of welcome to either Lucinda or Mrs. Patton.

"My mother and I are both so glad that you have come to stay in our home," Lord Adlington said quickly to fill the awkward silence. "Miss Leavitt, you adorn every room you enter with your beauty and wit."

"What a pretty compliment, my lord," Mrs. Patton simpered as if she were the recipient.

Lucinda forced herself not to blush. "Your estate is perfectly charming, my lord."

"Almost as charming as I am," Lord Adlington said with a teasing grin.

"Nothing could be," she assured him.

Lady Mary finally spoke, "I'll show you to your rooms now, Mrs. Patton and Miss Leavitt."

They followed Lady Mary through the main hall and up a staircase into the south wing. She showed them to a pair of rooms that overlooked the lake. The view was truly stunning.

"I will have the servants fetch your things and bring you some refreshments. And then you may rest before dinner," Lady Mary said.

Nothing the countess could have said would have endeared her more to Mrs. Patton, who was all smiles. Lucinda thanked her, but had no intention of wasting the afternoon in her bedchamber. She shut the door and was relieved to be without the presence of Mrs. Patton. Lucinda directed the maid as she unpacked her trunk, and then thanked her. Once the maid left, Lucinda put her bonnet back on and tied it. She tiptoed past Mrs. Patton's room and followed the hall around the corner, down a flight of stairs to an exterior door. She turned the knob and slipped out of the house.

The shining blue water of the lake was impossible for Lucinda to resist. She walked toward it and saw the small waves as they gently brushed the pebbled shore. The sun was high in the sky, and the image of Keynsham Hall reflected blurrily in the water. Lucinda took a deep breath. The air in the country was so much purer than the smog-filled air in London. She wondered again where her mother grew up. Had she lived in a city or in a town? Did she live near water? Who were her parents?

Lucinda felt hollow inside not knowing such little details about her mother's life. All she knew was that her mother had been a nursery maid for a business acquaintance of her father's. He'd met her, by chance, when one of her small charges had run into the dining room during a formal dinner. He'd always told Lucinda that he'd fallen in love with her mother at first sight. At least, he'd said this while her mother was still alive. Now, he never spoke of her. Never even said her name.

Taking another deep breath, Lucinda began skirting the edge of the lake. It was so abominably hot. Lucinda took out her handkerchief and pressed it against her damp forehead and neck, looking longingly at the cool water.

Lucinda glanced around the lake, then at the house. She did not see a soul.

"Why not?" she whispered aloud.

She sat down on an obliging tree stump and unlaced her boots. She pulled them off along with her sticky (and now stinky) stockings and wiggled her toes. Lucinda stood and walked gingerly on the pebbled beach before lifting her skirts and wading into the water. It felt glorious to feel the mud between her toes and the cold water up to her ankles.

"My, oh my, that's a great idea!"

Lucinda looked up to see a young woman around her own age with a narrow face, sharp features, and a pair of arresting gray eyes surrounded by light brown curls. The geometric design on her green skirt was the very latest in London fashion.

"The water is delightfully cool," Lucinda said.

"Then I shall join you," the stranger said in an American accent, taking a seat on the same stump and removing her own boots and stockings. She lifted her skirt with both hands and tiptoed from the beach into the lake.

"I know it is untoward in England to speak to a stranger without a formal introduction," the young lady said, "but I am afraid I am of a gregarious nature and cannot be quiet for so long a time. My name is Miss Persephone Merritt, and I am from New York City. That's in the United States of America."

"I could tell from your accent, and I quite like it," Lucinda said, holding out her hand. "My name is Miss Lucinda Leavitt, and I am from London."

Persephone released her hold on her skirt, allowing the hem to fall in the water. She took Lucinda's hand between her two warm ones and shook it vigorously.

"Delighted to make your acquaintance!" Persephone said a little too loudly, as she finally released Lucinda's hand. "I am here with my parents and my younger sister."

"Touring Europe?"

"No, just England."

"There are many places of historical interest, I believe," Lucinda offered.

Lucinda could see Persephone's color heighten. "We are not really here to see the sights, but to find me a suitable husband."

"Oh," Lucinda said. Before she could curb her tongue, she asked, "Why so far from home?"

Persephone bit her lip before responding. "I am afraid we are not genteel enough for our neighbors in New York City. My father acquired his fortune in railroads, but we are excluded by the local blue bloods. And our country is currently engaged in a civil war, so there are not many young men to be met at home. My parents are hoping to find me a good match in England where my background will not matter as much."

"Your background will always matter," Lucinda said bitterly. "But how much money you possess matters more."

Persephone nodded and waded out a little farther into the lake. "My family has been treated with such kindness here. We have only known the Adlingtons for a month, and they invited us to this weekend party. That would make those New York City socialites stare. The Merritts, guests of an earl."

"This is my first invitation to a house party as well," Lucinda said. "I have only recently left finishing school."

"I like you already," Persephone said in the same loud tone. "I hope we shall be friends."

Lucinda could only stare. She wondered if it was because the girl was an American—they were practically uncivilized there. Or perhaps it was Persephone's gregarious nature. To offer friendship so quickly, without ostentation . . . Lucinda had never experienced such openness. Nor had she any experience with friends of her own gender. To cover her own confusion, Lucinda bent over and touched her fingers into the water.

"Do you not wish to be my friend, Miss Leavitt?" Persephone asked bluntly.

This question propelled Lucinda back to standing. "I should be delighted to be your friend, Miss Merritt. Please, call me Lucinda."

"Persephone," she said. "Do you know Lord Adlington well?"

"Not really," Lucinda admitted. "His cousin is my father's business partner. I know his cousin well."

"Will he be here?"

"Who?"

"His cousin."

"Oh, David—Mr. Randall," Lucinda said. "I shouldn't think so. He's very busy at the office right now."

Persephone digested this. "*Mister* Randall. No title for the cousin, then?"

"No title. Only the son in line for the peerage can pass a title on to his children."

"So I would have to marry Lord Adlington to become an earl-ess."

Lucinda laughed. "There is no such thing as an earl-ess. An earl's wife's title is countess, but she is always addressed simply as *lady*. As in, Lady Mary Adlington."

"That seems rather complicated," Persephone said, wrinkling her nose.

"At least I learned something useful in finishing school."

"There you are, Persephone!" a voice cried from nearly halfway around the lake.

Lucinda turned to see another young woman who was undoubtedly Persephone's little sister; she had the same light brown hair styled in curls around her round face.

"You must come at once," she called out. "Mama is in a state. She wants Ingrid to start getting you dressed for dinner."

"I'm coming," Persephone said, and started to walk out of the water. The bottom ten inches of her dress were soaked. She didn't bother to put on her stockings but pulled on her boots and haphazardly tied the laces. She waved to Lucinda. "We will see each other very soon, my new friend."

Lucinda could not help but blush and smile as she waved back. "We will indeed, *friend*."

Nine

DAVID STRAIGHTENED HIS CRAVAT BEFORE buttoning his black dinner jacket. The underbutler opened the door to the parlor where the party was gathering. Every pair of eyes in the room, except one, turned to watch him enter. Lucinda did not have to turn around for David to know exactly who she was. He somehow knew the angle of her neck, the curve of her cheek as she smiled. At last, she glanced over her shoulder. Her eyes widened in recognition. Clearly Lucinda had not known he would be here.

"David, I was afraid you would not come after all," his mother said, standing next to his aunt.

David took his aunt's gloved hand and bent over it. "I am happy to be here, Lady Mary."

Alfred appeared at his side and clapped David on the back. "We almost went to dinner without you."

"I am sorry if I kept anyone waiting," David said.

"Nonsense," Alfred said jovially. "Come, allow me to introduce you to the rest of the party."

David followed Alfred to where an older couple stood by their two daughters—both girls had light brown hair and fresh, pretty faces.

"Mr. and Mrs. Merritt, and their lovely daughters, Miss Persephone and Miss Antigone. It is with great pleasure that I introduce you to my cousin, Mr. Randall. He's a businessman like yourself, Mr. Merritt."

David bowed formally.

"I know that you're already very well acquainted with Miss Leavitt," Alfred said with a knowing smile. "And her companion, Mrs. Patton."

Lucinda had been standing nearby, talking to one of the American girls. She was wearing the scarlet dress again that made her look magnificent. She curtsied gracefully and gave him an arch look. She held out her hand and he bent over it. Instead of releasing her hand, he tucked it through his arm and brought her with him as he followed his cousin to complete the introductions.

"Sir Thomas Hardin, Lady Althea Hardin, and their daughter, Miss Clara Hardin," Alfred said. "And David, you already know Mr. Tuttle and Mr. Silverman, which concludes our party."

He bowed to the ladies and nodded to the gentlemen.

Alfred clapped his hands together. "Let us go to dinner."

David placed his hand over Lucinda's on his arm. He wanted to make it very clear that he had chosen his dinner partner. Alfred escorted Miss Hardin, and Mr. Tuttle and Mr. Silverman each took one of the American girls. David pushed in Lucinda's chair and sat on the seat to the right of her. Miss Hardin sat on his right. David's mind wandered from the dinner back to the proposal from another firm to put up half the money in a speculation in South America.

"What are you thinking of, David?" Lucinda asked. "You seem distracted."

"I am being a poor dinner companion," David said. "My mind is taken up with a speculation from the Durham firm."

"Their projected numbers are sound," Lucinda said. "And if it is successful, your return on investment should be as much as fivefold."

"But it's a risk."

"Isn't all speculation a risk?"

"I suppose that is why they call it speculation," David said with a smile.

"No business talk at a dinner party, Cousin," Alfred complained.

"I am sure I know nothing about speculation," Miss Hardin said in her breathiest voice. "Or anything so unfeminine as business."

David supposed this last sentence was meant as a barb at

Lucinda. But when he looked at her, she was giving Miss Hardin a dazzling smile. "I assure you, Miss Hardin, that no one could possibly ever think that your head had any thoughts . . . of business. For my part, however, I think everyone, whether male or female, should be well acquainted with their own finances and how they are derived."

"Is that not a job for a lady's husband?" Mr. Tuttle asked.

"What if a lady has no husband?" Lucinda countered. "Whether she be unmarried or a widow, and then what? She would still need to understand her business affairs."

"A lady of *rank* will always have male relatives who can assist her in such matters," Miss Hardin said, her breathy voice sharp.

"Hear, hear," Sir Thomas said. "I would not want any daughter of mine to muddy her delicate mind with such matters."

"David, you're the businessman in the room," Alfred said. "What say you?"

David could feel the eyes of everyone on him, but only a pair of depthless blue ones mattered. "I am of the same mind as Miss Leavitt. A person should know as much as they can about their financial affairs. You never know whom you can wholly trust, even family."

"A sobering thought," Alfred said. "But this is a party! Aunt Randall, tell us all about the latest fashions in London."

David's mother was only too happy to oblige. The rest of the dinner passed without incident. The ladies left after the blood pudding to retire to another room, while the gentlemen drank their port. Alfred poured glasses for Merritt, Tuttle, Silverman, and Hardin. David poured his own drink. Merritt opened a fancy box of Cuban cigars and offered them to the members of the party, but David declined and walked over to the window for some fresh air. Alfred followed him.

"Perhaps I shall ask Miss Leavitt to tutor me in business," Alfred said. "She appears quite adept at it."

David felt a twinge of irritation. "Miss Leavitt, like her father, is gifted with numbers."

"But you must admit she is much nicer to look at, Cousin," Alfred said with a hearty laugh, clapping David on the back.

David hoped he managed something close to a smile.

"And if I were better with numbers, maybe I would not always be in debt," Alfred said.

"I will assist you in any way I can."

"No, no," Alfred said. "I will not take another farthing from you. I mean to stand on my own and to redeem all of the mortgages."

"How?"

"Marriage," Alfred said simply, "followed by moderate management."

"You mean to marry for money," David said.

"I've always known I would have to marry for money," Alfred said. "I suppose it's the lot of all peers saddled with estates they cannot afford to maintain. Lucky for me, there are plenty of lovely ladies with large dowries."

David gulped down his glass of port, feeling it burn the

inside of his throat. The thought of his cousin—or any man for that matter—marrying Lucinda for her money made him feel rather ill.

"Shall we join the ladies?" Mr. Silverman asked from the other side of the room.

David was only too happy to leave the smoke-filled room and the company of gentlemen.

The ladies were drinking tea. Lucinda sat with one of the Merritt girls at her side. Their conversation must have been amusing, for both young ladies were laughing. The other Merritt daughter sat by her mother. Miss Hardin was ensconced between David's mother and his aunt. She had a sneer in her expression; clearly she thought she had been awarded the most esteemed seating of the younger generation.

Lady Mary stood and greeted the gentlemen. She suggested they find a seat and enjoy their tea while the ladies presented their musical talents. Miss Hardin was the first asked to perform. She played a complicated classical piece on the piano. Alfred entreated her to play another, and for her second selection she played a minuet. The Merritt sisters were next. The younger one played the piano while the elder sister sang. Her voice was pure and pitch perfect. He even preferred it to the professional tenor that had performed in Bath. Lucinda clapped as loudly as the gentlemen. The Merritt sisters performed another song.

"Miss Leavitt, do you by chance play?" Lady Mary asked in a tone more suited for addressing a servant than a guest.

David blushed at his aunt's manners, but Lucinda did not show any sign of discomfort. She sat at the piano and pulled off her gloves. Her piece was not classical, nor complicated, and her voice did not have the purity of Miss Merritt's. Still, her simple country song captivated him in a way that the others had not. Even the insufferable Sir Thomas managed to be quiet during it.

"Thank you, Miss Leavitt," Lady Mary said.

"Will you not play another song, Miss Leavitt?" Alfred asked, obviously trying to draw attention from his mother's slight against her.

Lucinda stood and slid on her gloves slowly, one hand and then the other. "I shall stop while the audience is still clamoring for more."

David was walking toward Lucinda when his aunt asked him to join a hand of whist. He acquiesced and spent the rest of the evening at the card table watching Alfred flirt with both Lucinda and the elder Miss Merritt at the same time. He cringed every time he heard Lucinda's high laugh float across the room.

The next day they ate luncheon outside by the lake, at tables that had been set up underneath tents. Afterward, the male members of the party took turns lawn bowling. It came as no surprise to David when Lucinda, wearing a blue striped dress, asked to have a turn.

She threw the first ball and managed to miss the wooden pins entirely. Her second throw was marginally better, hitting one of the pins. Mr. Tuttle set the pin back up and Lucinda handed the bowling ball to the pretty American girl, Miss Persephone Merritt. She hurled the bowling ball and knocked down all the pins.

Lucinda walked toward the table where David stood. He handed her a glass of punch. She sipped it and said, "It appears that lawn bowling is not one of my talents."

"I would not add it to your list of accomplishments."

David saw his mother standing next to his aunt, and the Merritts were close by, watching the bowling game—all of the chaperones appeared to be occupied.

"Miss Leavitt, would you do me the honor of taking a stroll through the gardens with me?"

Lucinda looked from David to Mrs. Patton, who was busily devouring the cucumber sandwiches.

"I should like that very much, Mr. Randall."

David tucked her arm into his and began to leisurely walk from the open lawn by the lake to the entrance of a garden, surrounded by a large thicket that obscured its view from the rest of the party. David swung open the small iron gate for Lucinda and closed it again after they had passed through.

"This is truly a beautiful place," Lucinda said.

"Rather overgrown."

"I had noticed, but nothing that time and attention could not put to rights."

"Lucinda . . . ," David said. "I feel I must caution you against my cousin."

"Lord Adlington?" she said, the surprise in her tone obvious.

"Yes," David continued. "His finances are in an awful state, and I do not wish for you to be taken advantage of."

Lucinda turned her head away from him. "Am I so unattractive and ineligible that it is impossible for your cousin to sincerely attach himself to me?"

David placed his hand on her arm. "That is not my meaning at all. I simply wished to warn you that some of your suitors might have their eye on your fortune, and I should hate to see you taken in by a fortune hunter."

Lucinda brushed his hand off her arm. "Allow me some intelligence, David. I know exactly why each lady is here. The Misses Merritt are American heiresses, Miss Hardin's portion is rumored to be at least fifty thousand pounds, and I am the only child of a wealthy businessman. Your cousin obviously intends to marry one of us for our money in exchange for this historic estate and a title. It would not be the first, nor the last, of such bargains to be made."

"No, it would not."

"And I fail to see how my suitors are any concern of yours."

David cleared his throat. "I was only trying to look after you, as a friend."

"I don't want you to look after me. I'm very well able to look after myself!" Lucinda exclaimed. She pushed away from him, but stepped onto uneven ground, stumbled backward, and fell into a thornbush.

David offered his hand to help her up, but she waved him away, managing to get back on her feet without assistance. She tried to walk forward, but the back of her dress was hooked on several thorns. He watched her try to reach her hand around to where her dress was caught, but her arms were not long enough. She made a strange noise—something between a sob and a hysterical laugh—then buried her face in hands.

"Lucinda, are you all right?" David asked, concerned.

Lucinda's eyes peeked between her fingers, and he saw that she was laughing. She sobered long enough to say, "The irony of this situation is not lost on me."

"Would you like me to help you?"

"Please," she said with another giggle.

David stepped forward until his body was nearly touching hers. He carefully began to unhook each thorn from the back of Lucinda's dress.

"Try to come toward me slowly."

Lucinda took one small step forward, but could move no more. "I'm still caught on the bottom of my dress."

David took off his hat and swallowed as he moved closer to Lucinda. He tried to reach the thorns but couldn't, so he stepped closer still until their bodies were touching. He could feel her chest rise up and down quickly as she breathed. Laying one hand on her waist to steady himself, he leaned around her so he could see the thorns. With his other hand, he deftly unhooked the last four thorns that were holding her in place. He stood up straight, and as if they were waltzing, he led her by the waist away from the thicket.

His mind said to let her go, but his body wasn't listening. Her face was so close. Her lips looked so soft. He leaned in a little closer, his hand touching her shoulder.

"Ow," Lucinda said, biting her bottom lip.

David released her immediately and saw blood on the glove that had touched her shoulder.

"Lucinda, you're bleeding!"

She smirked. "David, I've told you before, do not underestimate my intelligence. I am very well aware I am bleeding."

David turned her around and saw that one of the thorns had ripped a large hole in the back of her dress, revealing a vicious scratch on her shoulder blade. He could even see the top of her corset. He averted his eyes, gazing pointedly at the sky as if he suddenly found clouds fascinating. He heard Lucinda laugh.

"It's only a shoulder, David," she said. "Everybody has one."

"I know—" he said, still avoiding her eyes . . . and her entire person.

"Two, in fact," Lucinda said.

Without looking at her, he pulled his handkerchief from his pocket and held it out in her direction. She laughed again at his expense before taking the handkerchief and pressing it against her opposite shoulder.

"I see them!" a loud American voice said.

Alfred and the elder Miss Merritt walked toward them. David stooped to pick up his hat and deftly placed it on his head.

"Miss Merritt and I have formed a search party," Alfred said genially. "Mrs. Patton was afraid that you two had become lost in the thicket."

"You are very close to the truth," Lucinda said, her arm still across her chest, holding his handkerchief to her opposite shoulder. "But more accurately, *I* fell into the thicket, and your poor cousin was forced to help me out of it again at the expense of his handkerchief and a scratch on my shoulder."

Miss Merritt released her hold on Alfred and stepped around Lucinda. "Poor dear! We had best get you to the house right away and tend to it. Mr. Randall, do you think it will need to be stitched? Lord Adlington, shall we fetch a doctor?"

Lucinda laughed. "It's only a scratch, Persephone."

Miss Merritt returned Lucinda's smile, and Alfred grinned at the pair.

"We don't want it to get infected, Lucinda," Miss Merritt said. "I am sure the housekeeper will have everything I need to tend it. Lord Adlington and Mr. Randall, would you please inform the rest of the party where we have gone to? I should hate it if poor Miss Hardin were to be forced to come searching for us."

"Not as much as I would," Lucinda muttered, and bid adieu to David and Alfred before following her friend on the path that led back to the house.

David dared one glance after them, giving him ample opportunity to glimpse her lovely uncovered shoulder. He gulped and looked back at his cousin.

Alfred raised his eyebrows. "I should have thought you knew your way around these gardens as well I do. We certainly played in here often enough as children."

"I—she—we—" David tried to explain, but nothing he said could wipe the smirk off Alfred's face.

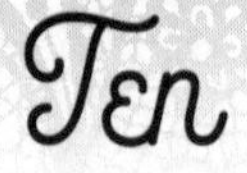

Ten

PERSEPHONE HELPED LUCINDA TAKE OFF her blue dress of iridescent striped silk. Lucinda gasped in pain as she lifted her arm above her shoulder. Persephone put her hand through the tear in the back of Lucinda's dress. "I am not sure your seamstress will be able to repair this rip. It's nearly eight inches long."

"It does not matter," Lucinda said.

Persephone placed the torn dress on a chair, then picked up a cloth and dipped it into the basin of water. She told Lucinda to turn and gently dabbed the cloth against Lucinda's scratch. Each touch stung and Lucinda bit her lip.

A knock sounded at the door, and Persephone called for them to come in. The housekeeper and the maid who had assisted Lucinda with dressing earlier stood in the doorway. Persephone directed them to place the talcum powder and the bandages on the washbasin stand.

"What a nasty scratch," the housekeeper said.

"But it is not as bad as it looks," Persephone said, and Lucinda stiffened when she felt her wipe the wound.

"Without all the blood, it is only a small cut," Persephone said.

She then instructed the housekeeper to hand her the talcum powder and the bandages. Persephone wrapped the bandage around Lucinda's shoulder and tied the ends into a tight knot. She dismissed the housekeeper and the maid, who took the soiled dress and the bloodstained cloth out to wash.

"I will wash and change that bandage for you tomorrow," Persephone said. "It's important that it stays clean. Now, shall I help you into another dress, or would you like to lie down?"

"Another dress," Lucinda said. "I do not sleep during the day."

Persephone opened the wardrobe containing Lucinda's belongings and selected a yellow gingham day dress with a row of circular yellow buttons down the front. She eased the dress over her sore shoulder, and Lucinda buttoned it up.

"There, you look as pretty as a picture," Persephone said. "Shall we return to the party?"

"I'd rather not," Lucinda admitted.

"I don't wonder! That Miss Hardin sure puts on airs, and her father is only a little baron," Persephone said.

"A *what*?"

"Baronet—little baron."

"I'm not sure that's what 'baronet' means."

"You English and your silly titles," Persephone said, shaking her head. "I'm glad at least baronets' daughters don't have titles. That Miss Hardin is insufferable enough as she is."

"This is Miss Hardin attempting to be civil," Lucinda said. "At school she never bothered with appearances. She was meaner than an old cat with its tail cut off."

Persephone giggled. "You know what I should like to do?"

"What?"

"See the view from the roof. I daresay we could see for miles in every direction. Besides, there is something so romantic about roofs in all the stories I've ever read. Do you like to read novels?"

"I adore novels," Lucinda said. "Have you read *She Knew She Was Right*?"

"Yes!" Persephone said loudly in her very American accent. "I read it in *Harper's Weekly*, and I was ever so disappointed the author died without finishing the novel. Although I am sure Eurydice would have picked Mr. Thisbe in the end. He was such a kind and steady man. And so devoutly religious, unlike the worldly Lord Dunstan."

"I mean to discover the identity of the deceased author and see if any of her family members knew how she would have ended the story."

"I knew I liked you!" Persephone exclaimed, embracing her. "Golly, what a capital idea!"

Lucinda stiffened, but returned the embrace. "Let us find the roof."

Persephone linked arms with Lucinda as they left her room. They made several wrong turns and passed through a long hall with a picture gallery. The gentleman in the second to last portrait bore a marked resemblance to David. Lucinda unconsciously stopped before it.

"He could be Mr. Randall's twin, couldn't he?" Persephone said. "Except the eyes are different."

"Yes," Lucinda agreed. "Mr. Randall's eyes are larger and not so close set."

"Mr. Randall is sure handsome," Persephone remarked meaningfully.

Lucinda only nodded and led her newest—and only—female friend past the portrait gallery and up several flights of stairs that appeared to be neglected. The bottom of their skirts were covered in dust before they found the door that led to the roof. Lucinda gave the door a push, and they felt a rush of fresh air with a slight breeze in the otherwise oppressive summer heat when it opened.

Lucinda stepped gingerly out onto the roof tiles, but Persephone walked without any hesitation. She pointed out a small village in the distance and another smaller estate not far from it.

They walked to the other side of the roof, which afforded a view of the lake. Lucinda could not see any of the ladies of the party; they had probably all retired to the house to rest before dinner. But David's tall, straight form was easily distinguishable, as well as his cousin's slightly smaller one. She watched as David tossed a stone into the lake, where it skipped a couple times on the water's surface before sinking. Lord Adlington threw his stone and it skipped three times.

Persephone's eyes must have followed Lucinda's, for she said, "They are nice young men, aren't they?"

"Yes," was all Lucinda managed to say.

"I suppose neither would be interested in me without my father's fortune," Persephone said bluntly.

"Or my father's fortune," Lucinda admitted. "My mother was a nursery maid before she married my father, and he started life as a street sweeper in London."

Lucinda watched her new friend closely to see how she reacted to this information, but Persephone's face did not evince any surprise or dismay. Quite the reverse; she smiled broadly and said, "Then we are both adventuresses, seeking to raise our fortunes!"

"Except we are the ones with the fortunes and the men have the titles," Lucinda said.

Persephone laughed. "Which young man do you prefer?"

Lucinda flushed and turned away from the Randall cousins to look at the sun setting on the opposite side of the house. "I have no claim on either. And I am not entirely sure if I want to marry."

"Why ever not?"

"I'm not overfond of running a household," Lucinda

said. "I much prefer the pace and the pressure of business. If it were possible, I should like to take a place in my father's countinghouse. I am rather good with numbers."

"Perhaps I should be more direct," Persephone pressed. "Do you have any designs on Lord Adlington?"

"No," Lucinda said quickly. "None at all."

"I like him very much," Persephone said with her American bluntness. "And I have a shrewd suspicion that my father's fortune is just what this old house needs."

"I wish you every success," Lucinda said, unsure of how to respond to such openness.

Persephone gave a loud laugh and tucked her arm back into Lucinda's. Lucinda steeled herself not to flinch at being touched. She liked it—she just wasn't used to it.

"We had best find our way back to your bedchamber and get dressed for dinner. And even though you did not tell me, I have another shrewd suspicion," Persephone said.

"What is that?"

"That you and your Mr. Randall did not tell the entire story of the thornbush."

It was a good thing that Lucinda was leaving in the morning. She had already ruined two dresses on this house visit, and she had only packed one other day dress. The maid assisted Lucinda into the dark green silk dress with small sleeves and trimmed with a golden fringe. It had three large flounces in the skirt and a large bow in the back. She pulled the collar higher to cover the white bandage on her shoulder. The maid combed and arranged Lucinda's dark locks, then handed her a lace shawl to go over her shoulders. The shawl covered the bandage better than the collar of the dress. Lucinda thanked the maid and walked from the south wing to the main wing where the formal rooms were located.

The underbutler opened the door to the main parlor. Lucinda walked in to discover the room had only two occupants—Lord Adlington and Persephone, in close conversation. They both stepped back from the other and greeted her warmly. Lucinda raised her eyebrows suggestively at Persephone, who only smiled in return.

The door opened again, and several more members of the party entered the spacious gathering room, including Miss Hardin. She lifted her chin higher when she saw Lucinda. She stepped lightly toward the three of them and said in a poisonous tone, "My dear Miss Leavitt, I would have thought your wound from this afternoon would have kept you in your bed."

"I am much recovered, Miss Hardin," Lucinda said.

"No doubt owing to your *common* constitution," she sneered.

Lucinda felt the barb about her birth, but said lightly, "I am sure the credit of my recovery belongs to Miss Persephone Merritt. She kindly tended my scratch."

"Miss Merritt, you aspire to be a nurse for Miss Leavitt? Very fitting for *your* circumstances and background."

David entered the room then and began to walk toward

Lucinda, as if coming to claim her for his dinner partner, when Miss Hardin stood directly in his path. "Mr. Randall, I have not had an opportunity to speak with you all day," Miss Hardin said in a pouty voice. "Would you be so kind as to escort me to dinner?"

David glanced over Miss Hardin's head at Lucinda. "It would be my privilege, Miss Hardin," he said formally.

Miss Hardin did not wait for David to offer it before she slid her hand through his arm and held it tightly. She skillfully turned him away from Lucinda and the Merritts and directed him to the other side of the room, where her parents stood, ensuring that David's back was to the rest of the party. Lucinda could not hear what they spoke of, but Miss Hardin gave several high, girlish laughs.

When dinner was announced, Mr. Tuttle offered his escort to Lucinda. She accepted it. He assisted her to her seat on the opposite end of the table from David, Mr. Silverman on her other side. Mr. Silverman rivaled Mrs. Patton with his attention to eating, and Mr. Tuttle's banal conversation consisted entirely of recounting his sporting experiences in the game of cricket with excruciating detail. For once, Lucinda did not mind being dismissed with the ladies so the gentlemen could drink and smoke in masculine solitude.

"Shall we have dancing tonight, Miss Merritt? I confess myself eager to learn your steps," Alfred said later, after the gentlemen had rejoined them. "Mother, will you play for us?"

Lady Mary sniffed. "I am afraid, Alfred, that I am much too fatigued."

"Dear Alfred, I shall be happy to take her place," Mrs. Randall said, and immediately stood and went to the piano.

David opened it for his mother, and Mrs. Randall began to play a lively Scottish tune. Lord Adlington led Persephone to the center of the room and they began to dance. David caught Lucinda's eye just as Mr. Tuttle asked her to be his dance partner. Lucinda accepted graciously, but indulged in a sigh worthy of Mrs. Patton. It did not surprise her to see David escorting Miss Hardin to join the set.

Mrs. Randall played very well and the dancers all knew their parts. Lucinda thought she might have enjoyed it if David were her partner, and if every time she lifted her arm it did not ache. Lucinda bowed to Mr. Tuttle and thanked him for the dance. Mrs. Randall began to play another tune and Mr. Tuttle asked Lucinda if she would dance the next with him.

"I am sorry, but I shall have to excuse myself," Lucinda said. "My shoulder is still rather sore, but I believe Miss Antigone would be a most excellent partner."

Mr. Tuttle bowed and did indeed solicit Antigone's hand. Lucinda sat on a sofa, which afforded an excellent view of the room. She hoped that David would sit beside her, but Miss Hardin firmly led him to join yet another dancing set. Lucinda was forced to watch David dance with Miss Hardin once more, before she told Mrs. Patton she felt unwell. Mrs. Patton solicitously led Lucinda to her bedchamber and rang for a maid.

Once Lucinda was dressed for bed, she turned off her gas lamp and closed her eyes. But sleep eluded her. Her mind buzzed with thoughts, like a bee circling a flower. The easiest thought to digest was one of gratitude. After a lifetime of isolation by circumstance and uncertain social class, she had found a true friend in Persephone Merritt. One who did not care about her background, one who was loyal. *Perhaps to a fault,* Lucinda thought as she remembered Persephone's sharp defense of her to Miss Hardin. Her sister, Antigone, was equally kind.

Lucinda wondered if she could ever be truly comfortable or happy in high society. How long would she have to endure the barbs from the likes of Miss Hardin or the cold indifference of Lady Mary before she would be accepted as one of them? Or, like at finishing school, would she never be accepted at all?

But her most pressing fear was that this entire disaster of a house visit would be for naught. What if Mrs. Smith's relatives in Shaftesbury didn't know what her intentions were for her fictional characters? What if Mrs. Smith hadn't kept notes? Lucinda would have suffered the snubs and humiliations of Miss Hardin and Lady Mary without being any closer to discovering Eurydice's final choice. Her ultimate decision between her two suitors: Lord Dunstan and Mr. Thisbe.

And the last thought was like a bee sting on her heart: the

image of David dancing with Miss Hardin. She swatted it away from her mind. But the thought kept buzzing back, and each time it left a stinger. Lucinda turned to lie on her stomach and pulled the pillow over her head.

Why did she care if David danced with Miss Hardin? She hated Clara, of course; she was cruel for no reason other than the fact that she could be. But a niggling thought in the back of her head told Lucinda that she would have resented David dancing with *any* woman. Which was ridiculous! He was free to dance with whomever he liked—it wasn't as if Lucinda had nor even *wanted* any claim over him.

Lucinda threw the pillow off the bed and flopped onto her back, kicking at the coverlet. Why couldn't she stop thinking and go to sleep?

She brought her hand to her face and traced her bottom lip with her pointer finger. For a moment, in the thornbushes, she'd thought David was going to kiss her. She couldn't help but wonder what it would have felt like if he had.

Eleven

LUCINDA WAS THE STUBBORNEST, MOST headstrong, most infuriating young lady David had ever met. And yet he could not stop thinking about her or their almost-kiss when he'd helped her out of the thornbushes. The thrill of her body pressed against his. Seeing her beautiful bare shoulder. He couldn't breathe just thinking about it.

"I don't want you to look after me. I'm very well able to look after myself!" she had said.

He believed she was. If anyone was capable of looking after their own interests, it was Lucinda Leavitt. Then why did he have the overwhelming urge to try to assist her, to be near her? She was not like other young ladies. She did not want him to shoulder her burdens. She did not appreciate him offering his advice. Nor did she care much for flowers or frip-peries. No, the blasted young woman only liked two things: numbers and novels.

Novels.

David couldn't help but grin when he thought of her determination to discover the ending of *She Knew She Was Right*. That title certainly described Lucinda.

"That's it," he said aloud. He would give her a new book.

"What's it?" his mother inquired pleasantly.

David flushed. "Nothing. Shall you accompany me, Mother?"

"No, dearest," she said. "I believe I should stay here a little longer and help your aunt. The house party has greatly wea-ried her, and all of their financial difficulties prey heavily upon her mind."

"I hope you'll be able to help her."

"I'm sure I shall," his mother said. "Now give me a kiss, and I shall see you in a fortnight."

David directed a servant to bring down his portmanteau and took leave of his aunt. He then sent for a carriage, and just when it pulled up in front of the house, Lucinda came out-side to the sultry heat of the morning. She was dressed in a black skirt with a white blouse and a black jacket with puffed sleeves, the ensemble emphasizing her narrow waist. She looked as cool as a cucumber and perfectly delectable.

David swallowed loudly. "Should you like to share my car-riage to the station?"

"Yes, please," Lucinda said with a sunny smile. "If you don't mind making a short stop in Shaftesbury."

"To visit the Smiths?"

"Of course."

Mrs. Patton came outside and said, "Lucinda, how many times do I have to remind you that you cannot go out in public without me?"

"I forgot—again," Lucinda said. "Mr. Randall has kindly offered to share his carriage to the train station."

"How very thoughtful of you, Mr. Randall," Mrs. Patton said in a sweet voice.

"I enjoy your company," David said, and then asked a groom to put their trunks on the carriage. He next assisted Mrs. Patton and Lucinda into the carriage before hopping in himself.

"Miss Leavitt, how did you enjoy the party?" David asked formally.

"The party was memorable," Lucinda said. "And the house was like stepping into a history lesson. The beautiful arches. The soaring ceilings. They do not build houses like that anymore."

"No, they do not," David agreed. "Should you like to live in such a house?"

Mrs. Patton offered her unsolicited opinion. "I should think any young lady would be pleased to live in such a house."

"Not this young lady," Lucinda said.

"Why not, Lucinda?" Mrs. Patton inquired.

"It's simply too large, too cumbersome," Lucinda explained.

"Three-quarters of the house is never in use. The estate would always be a financial burden—a drain on your income. It doesn't make sense fiscally."

"But the beauty of the countryside—" Mrs. Patton pressed.

"Does Miss Leavitt prefer London?" David asked.

"I love London, for London is home," Lucinda said. "But someday I should very much like a snug little house on a manageably sized estate in the country to escape the polluted air of London."

Mrs. Patton sat up at this. "Yes, yes. The air in London, particularly in the winter, is so very bad. I cannot breathe without placing a handkerchief over my mouth whenever I venture outdoors."

David listened to Mrs. Patton compare the benefits of living in the country compared to the city for half an hour. The coachman, as directed, stopped at the post office in Shaftesbury.

"Are we at the train station?" Mrs. Patton asked.

"No, we are at the post office in Shaftesbury," David replied, trying to suppress a smile. "I have a small item of business to conduct here."

Lucinda sat forward eagerly. "Let us go in at once."

David helped both ladies from the carriage and opened the pointed-arch door to the post office—a tall stone building with two gables. The building's windows did not provide much light, and the air felt musty. A clerk with receding brown hair and narrow-framed spectacles addressed them. "And how may I help you today, sir?"

"We are looking for the Smiths who recently visited Bath.

Would you be so good as to give us their direction?" David asked.

The clerk pushed his spectacles up his nose and peered closely at Lucinda. "We are not supposed to share the private information of our customers."

"But—" David began.

Lucinda cut him off. "Of course you aren't. I am impressed by your integrity, sir."

The clerk flushed and stammered, "J-just—just doing me duty, miss."

Lucinda held out her hand to David, and he took it in his own. She immediately pulled her hand away, and he looked at her, confused.

"I'm not trying to hold your hand," she said out of the side of her mouth. "I need your coin purse."

"Whatever for?"

"Money, obviously."

"Oh."

He pulled his purse out of his jacket pocket and placed it in her hand. Lucinda opened it and took out two shillings, then placed them on top of the desk. "We do not wish you to get into any trouble. If you would just be so kind as to give us the general direction to the Smiths' home, no private information—only what anyone in the street would say—we will bid you good day."

The clerk picked up the two coins and rubbed them together between his thumb and his pointer finger.

"If you were to ask at the pub," the clerk began, "they'd

tell you to continue north on this road and take the first right turn onto Wincombe Lane. About three or so miles down it, you'll be able to see a large house on the south side of the road—Wincombe Park. That's the home of the Smiths."

"Thank you," Lucinda said with a flirtatious smile.

"Good day," David said. He touched the brim of his hat with his finger and slightly inclined his head.

David escorted both ladies back to the carriage and directed the driver toward Wincombe Lane. After a quarter of an hour, Lucinda stuck her head out the window to look for Wincombe Park. A great gust of wind blew by, and she was forced to hold on to her bonnet with her hands. Sheepishly, she ducked back into the carriage and sat in her seat. David could not help but laugh, and Lucinda joined in his mirth. Mrs. Patton tutted and mumbled something about ladylike behavior that neither Lucinda nor David paid any heed to. David did so love to hear Lucinda laugh.

Lucinda blushed and began to finger the brooch pinned to the collar of her shirt. David blinked, suddenly realizing how intensely he had been staring at her face. His eyes traveled to the oval golden brooch at her throat; etched in white stone was the profile of a woman. He was not close enough to see the fine details, but the shape of the woman's face reminded him of Lucinda's.

"Is the brooch a likeness of your mother?"

Lucinda nodded. "She gave it to me the Christmas before she died. Everyone who knew her says that I greatly resemble her, but I am afraid that her face has faded from my memories. It's as if they have darkened with age."

David paused before saying, "My elder brother, Francis, died when I was only five years old. He was ten years my senior. And sometimes I wonder if I really remember him, or if I just remember what my father told me about him."

Francis, the perfect son. *If only you could be more like Francis,* his father always said. And David had always added in his head, *and less like yourself.*

"I suppose it's our stories that keep our lost loved ones alive," Lucinda said thoughtfully. "You are fortunate that your father was able to speak of Francis. My father cannot endure even my mother's name being mentioned, let alone any anecdotes about her personality or the things she liked. After she died, he took her portrait down. We moved houses. He hired new servants. It was as if she never existed."

"I believe your father loved your mother very much," David said. "My father told my mother that he was shattered after her death."

"So was I," Lucinda said. "And now that she is never spoken of, she feels so very gone all the more."

"What was her name?"

"Jane."

"Jane," David said in a soft tone. "A lovely name."

Lucinda gave him a sad smile and again looked out the carriage window in search of the Smiths' house. David watched as Mrs. Patton's head bobbed forward and back. Her eyes would close as her head leaned forward, and then her eyes would snap back open as her head fell back. Mrs. Patton's head bobbed for several minutes before it slumped forward and David could hear the steady repetition of her snoring. Lucinda continued to stare raptly out the window.

"I see it. There!" Lucinda said, pointing to a tall house, the roof barely visible behind a thicket of trees.

The coach driver must have also seen it, for he turned the carriage down a winding gravel lane that led up to the house. David did not need to lean out the window like Lucinda to get a good view of it. The house had a large stone tower in the center that was flanked on both sides by Tudor-style gables, painted white with brown wooden trim placed in rectangular sections. The closest gable had a bay window with a copper roof. It was an odd mix of a historic building with contemporary renovations.

When the carriage came to a halt, David looked from the sleeping Mrs. Patton to Lucinda, who pressed a finger to her lips and shook her head. David nodded. He quietly exited the carriage and then placed his hands around Lucinda's trim waist and lifted her out. Such a small exertion should not have left him feeling breathless, but it did. He could hear Lucinda also breathing quickly in and out.

"Well. That is one way to get out of a carriage," she said. "Next time, a simple hand of assistance should do quite nicely."

David laughed and offered his arm. Lucinda took it, and they walked toward the arched door in the center of the stone tower. David knocked loudly with his cane, and they waited several moments before a young maid opened the door.

She seemed surprised to see them, and David handed her his card and requested to meet the owner of the house. The maid took the card and bobbed an awkward curtsy before running back down the hall. David looked at Lucinda, and she shrugged her lovely shoulders. They were kept waiting for several minutes before the young maid returned with an elderly matron wearing a gray-and-white striped dress and a white lace cap.

At first David thought the matron was the housekeeper, but then she introduced herself as the owner of the house. David bowed and introduced himself and Lucinda.

"I won't stand at points with strangers," the matron said. "Are you come to inquire about the house?"

"No, I am afraid not," David said.

"If you are not here about purchasing the house, then what business brings you to Wincombe Park?" she asked bluntly.

Lucinda stepped forward. "We are looking for the family of Mrs. Smith."

"Mrs. Smith?" the matron asked incredulously. "What would fashionable young people likes yourselves want with a Mrs. Smith?"

"We are trying to locate the family of the recently deceased author Mrs. Smith," Lucinda explained.

"Well, they ain't here."

“Are you sure?” Lucinda asked.

“Dead sure,” the matron said. She stubbed a fat thumb at her sagging bosom. “I is Mrs. Smith, and I sure as stone ain’t dead.”

David coughed. “It appears we have made a mistake. We apologize for taking up so much of your valuable time, Mrs. Smith.”

“I should’ve known fancy folks like you wouldn’t be interested in this old house,” Mrs. Smith huffed.

“No, no. I think it is a lovely house,” Lucinda said hurriedly. “Are you obliged to sell it?”

“My husband died not a fortnight ago, and I discovered he was dead broke. I can no longer afford to live here or pay for the servants. That’s why all I’ve got left by way of help is Sally here, and precious little help she is.”

The young maid shrank into the shadow of the wall at her mistress’s words.

David cleared his throat. “Mrs. Smith, our condolences on the death of your husband, and our best wishes for a speedy sale of your house.”

David took the matron’s hand and bent over it. Lucinda gave the lady a curtsy and then took his arm. He handed her into the carriage, where Mrs. Patton still sat snoring, then directed the driver to take them to the train station. He climbed into the carriage and saw that Lucinda was no longer sitting next to her chaperone, but on the side of the coach that faced forward. David sat next to her, his shoulder gently bumping the puffed sleeve of her jacket.

"What an odd house and an even odder occupant," David remarked.

Lucinda giggled. "I liked them both."

David flashed her a grin and then sobered. "I am sorry we have reached another dead end in our search for the author's identity and her family."

Lucinda played with her hands in her lap. "It was no great matter after all . . . Just a silly story."

David placed his hands over hers to stop their movement. Lucinda looked up into his eyes.

"If it matters to you, then it is not silly," he said.

"You are a true friend, David," she replied warmly. Her voice sounded breathless again, her face so close to his. He found himself looking at her lips as she licked them. She was near enough to kiss. He swallowed and forced himself to lean away from her. He released her hands and resolutely looked out the opposite window of the carriage.

Twelve

THE GASLIGHT FIXTURES MADE LONG shadows all over the room as Lucinda dipped the pen in the ink bottle and then began writing the thirtieth, nearly identical, letter:

Dear Mr. and Mrs. Porter,

I believe you stayed at No. 15 Laura Place sometime between the months of January and March earlier this year. Mrs. B. Smith, deceased author of She Knew She Was Right, was also a guest of the boardinghouse at that time. Did you, by chance, meet her? Or do you have any pertinent information about her family or know the direction of her permanent residence? Or where she was buried?

I am trying to locate whoever is in possession of her final papers. Thank you for your time and assistance in this matter.

Yours sincerely,
L. Leavitt
London

Lucinda sprinkled a little sand on the paper to help dry the ink and then blew it off. She folded the letter, carefully poured a little sealing wax on the pointed edge, then pressed the Leavitt seal to close it. It took several minutes for the sealing wax to harden before she turned the letter over and wrote the direction for Mr. and Mrs. Porter residing in Kent, then placed it on top of her stack of letters to take to the penny post.

Lucinda picked up her pen and carefully put a checkmark next to the Porters' names. There was only one pair of boarders left: Mrs. Burntwood and her personal companion. She picked up yet another piece of paper and began writing, "Dear Mrs. Burntwood . . ."

Once finished, Lucinda placed the very last letter on the top of the precariously tall stack with satisfaction, then picked up the bell and rang for the butler. Mr. Ruffles arrived in the sitting room in less than a minute.

Lucinda gathered up her letters and handed them to him.

"Please see that these go out first thing in the morning, Ruffles."

"Yes, miss."

"Thank you," Lucinda said, then added, "Has my father come home yet?"

"Yes, miss," Mr. Ruffles replied. "He's in his study."

She nodded and waited for him to leave the room before chewing on her thumbnail. Was now the right time to talk to him?

"Lucinda, dear," Mrs. Patton said in a singsong voice. "A lady never bites her fingernails."

Lucinda took her thumbnail out of her mouth. "Thank you for the reminder, Mrs. Patton. I am going to speak to my father about an important matter."

Mrs. Patton sighed and set down her embroidery. "Lucinda, your father is a very busy man, and it isn't ladylike for one to put themselves forward." She patted the seat next to her. "Why don't you come help me with my embroidery, dear girl? You have such neat little stitches."

Lucinda shook her head. "I am afraid the gas lamp does not give off enough light," she said, feigning a yawn. "And I am so tired."

"Go to bed, dear girl," Mrs. Patton said. She pointed her needle at Lucinda as she said in the same singsong voice, "A lady needs her beauty rest."

Lucinda pursed her lips and nodded as she stood. She closed the door to the sitting room and walked away from the stairs that led to her bedchamber, heading instead toward her father's study. Trying to gain some freedom in her life was making her a pathological liar. She knocked lightly on the door of the study.

"Come in," her father said.

Lucinda walked into the dimly lit room. The gaslights highlighted the wrinkles and lines on her father's face. He looked so tired. So old.

"You missed dinner, Father."

"Very busy right now at the office, Lucy," her father said without looking up from the paper in his hand. "We are in the middle of negotiating an important speculation opportunity."

"The Durham project?"

This made him look up, if only momentarily. "Yes." He set down the paper and picked up his pen, dipped it in the inkwell, and began to write.

"Mr. Randall told me about it," Lucinda said.

"Eh?" he said as he continued to write.

"I was thinking if it is improper for me to be at the counting-house," Lucinda began, "then I could work from home."

He dipped his pen again and continued to write without looking up at her.

"You've been coming home later and later every night," Lucinda said quickly. "I know there is so much work to do, and I am sure I could help you, Father."

He shook his head slowly. His mouth was tight, his jaw clenched.

"I want to help you with the business."

"We are not having this discussion again," he said, still not looking at her.

"It isn't a discussion if only one side is allowed to argue their opinion," Lucinda said, clenching her fists.

"Go to bed, Lucy."

"How can we have a discussion when you never even look at me?" Lucinda asked, tears of frustration forming in her eyes. She pressed her hands against her chest. "Let alone try to see me for who I really am. I am not my mother, and I do not want the future you and she planned out for me."

Her father set down the pen and, for the first time since she came home from school, he truly looked at her.

"You will not speak of your mother in that way," he said through clenched teeth. "Now leave!"

Lucinda turned and fled the room, tears freely falling from her eyes. Not tears of sadness, but ones of rage. An impossible anger made her chest burn and her hands shake. She would find a way out of this pretty cage, and she didn't care how many lies she would have to tell to do it.

Thirteen

A FORTNIGHT LATER, LUCINDA WAS sitting at the front window again, counting the bricks on the house across the street, waiting for the post to arrive. She'd already received six replies from the thirty letters she'd sent out inquiring after Mrs. Smith. Unfortunately, the six people who had taken the time to respond had no recollection of meeting anyone named Mrs. Smith while staying in Bath. Still, there were twenty-four more possible replies, and she had not yet given up hope of finding the author's relations.

Lucinda's yawn turned into a sigh. She was, however, starting to give up on hoping her father would ever relent about letting her work for the company. Even worse, since her outburst in his study, her father had steadily avoided her. Every night, he either stayed late at his office or ate dinner at his club, leaving Lucinda alone with only Mrs. Patton for company.

The postman took off his hat and waved at Lucinda through the window. She ran to the door and opened it. He handed her the post and smiled at her like an old friend. "Good day, miss."

The top letter was addressed to L. Leavitt. She looked up at the postman and grinned. "It is a good day. Thank you, sir."

She closed the door and put the top letter in her apron pocket. She riffled through the other letters and found another for her, from Persephone. She smiled and placed it in her pocket as well. The rest of the letters she handed over to Mr. Ruffles, who stood next to her, patiently waiting to receive them. He opened the door to the sitting room for her. Inside, Mrs. Patton was asleep, sitting up on the sofa, her head bobbing lightly up and down with her breathing.

Lucinda sat on the chaise, as far away from Mrs. Patton as possible. She pulled Persephone's letter out of her pocket, broke the seal, and opened it:

Dear Lucinda,

How I wish you could have accompanied us to Brighton and shared in all of our adventures! I am sure you would have loved to come sea bathing with me. The ladies have to enter the water through a bathing machine (a little house on wheels) where I changed into my bathing dress, and the attendant tied a cord around my waist so I wouldn't float away. What a lark!

We are staying in a hotel across the street from the Royal Pavilion and it looks like something out of a book with all of its domes and minarets. Lord Adlington says it resembles a fancy cake more than it does a royal palace. But I confess, I find it fascinating, just like the wicked Prince Regent who built it. The Pavilion is now owned by the city of Brighton and the royal stables have been converted to a concert hall. My family attended a concert there only last night with Lord Adlington.

Lord Adlington has grown most particular in his attentions to me and has even asked me to call him by his given name—Alfred. I must confess to you that I like him more and more every time I see him—and I see him quite a lot! Each morning we walk on the beach with Antigone, who sends you her warmest regards.

I hope you are doing well, and I can't wait until we come back to London and I see you again.

Your friend,
Persephone Merritt

P.S. I still want to hear the full story of the thornbush.

Lucinda couldn't help but laugh as she read her friend's descriptions of sea bathing and a certain earl they both knew. She was still smiling to herself as she folded the pages back together.

The second letter was lighter than the first. A single sheet of paper. Nervously, Lucinda chewed on her thumbnail. What if it was nothing again? She didn't need another disappointment. She stared at the letter for over a minute before she ran her thumb underneath the seal and opened it. The page contained only a short missive in an elaborately ornate hand:

Dear Mr. B. Beavitt,

Pay me a visit if you wish to know more of the author Mrs. Smith.

Mrs. Burntwood
Burntwood Folly
Reading, Berkshire

The extra flourish at the end of every word was identical to the letter Mr. Gibbs had shown her in the office.

Lucinda clasped the letter to her chest. She couldn't get enough air, her chest straining against her tight corset: She'd finally found the person who sent the final pages of *She Knew She Was Right* to the editor!

Lucinda slumped back in the chair and read the letter once more. It contained only one cryptic line, but it was enough to restore hope.

Mr. Ruffles opened the door to the sitting room and announced, "Mr. Randall."

Both Lucinda and Mrs. Patton scrambled to their feet, Mrs. Patton covering a yawn with her hand. David strode into the room as if he owned the house. His brown hair was slightly disheveled, and his leather bag was stuffed full of papers. He bowed to both ladies, but his brown eyes were on Lucinda.

"Do sit down," Lucinda and Mrs. Patton said in unison.

David carefully placed his leather bag on the table and pulled out a small brown package before taking a seat on the chaise next to Lucinda. He handed the package to her. "For you."

"Thank you," Lucinda said, taking the package from his

hand. She untied the twine and unwrapped the brown paper. Inside was a newly bound red leather volume. She turned the book to its spine and read aloud: "*East and West* by Mrs. Smith. It's one of my favorite works; I did not even know it was available in book form. Thank you so much!"

"Mr. Gibbs said that it isn't for sale for another month," David said. "I thought you might enjoy receiving the very first copy."

"I do!" Lucinda said, caressing the cover of the book. "It is the most thoughtful gift I have ever received."

David smiled at her and she felt breathless again, as if her corset strings were tied rather too tight.

"It certainly has a handsome binding," Mrs. Patton said from across the room.

"And you brought more business papers for *my father* to look at?" Lucinda prompted.

"Yes," David said. "More of what you—your father has been doing. Checking numbers, making sure they are correct, and comparing them with our own estimates. We hope to have the Durham speculation signed and completed in the next month."

"I can certainly tell my father to do that."

"He is free to add any notes or suggestions you or he may have to the contracts in the margins," David said. "These are only the roughs; we will have a clerk write the final ones out in law hand."

"I am not at all sure why you are not telling Mr. Leavitt

directly about this," Mrs. Patton said. "So much talk of business can be damaging to a young lady's delicate constitution."

Lucinda swallowed the retort that she was not at all delicate. But it was useless to fight with Mrs. Patton. She would only give a long sigh and repeat her usual advice.

David, surprisingly, came to her defense. "Miss Leavitt is one the most intelligent people I have ever met, and I believe she is more than capable of doing what I've asked of her. And I must also add that she is lucky to have your care and support."

Mrs. Patton's thin, sallow cheeks showed a little blush. "I treat her as if she were my own daughter."

"Miss Leavitt is so blessed to have you as a companion," he said, the charmer.

Miss Leavitt did not agree, but she put on a civil smile nevertheless. "I have a surprise for you as well, Mr. Randall. And it is as wonderful as your book."

"Are you sure?" he asked shrewdly. "It is *leather-bound*."

Lucinda handed David the letter and whispered, "I have finally found someone who knew Mrs. Smith. We might be hours away from knowing the true ending."

David read the letter. "How appropriate that the person is from Reading."

"It is pronounced 'Redding,'" Mrs. Patton said primly as she looked up from her embroidery.

"When can we set out for Reading?" Lucinda asked brightly. "I am sure *my father* is very eager to have this business matter resolved."

David shook his head. "I am afraid I cannot leave London for at least a week. I am too far behind with my work as it is."

Lucinda folded her arms. A week was much too long. She'd already waited a fortnight. "Then I will leave tomorrow without you."

"You cannot travel unattended," David protested.

"Mrs. Patton is my chaperone; I need no other. I am sure my father will agree," Lucinda said, and added to herself, *I don't need* any *escort!*

"But, Lucinda—" Mrs. Patton protested.

"We shall take the early train," Lucinda said.

David stood. "I should go—allow you time to pack."

Lucinda got to her feet, still cradling the leather-bound book in one arm. "Thank you so much for the book and for the papers. You . . . you are a true friend," she said, holding out her other hand.

He didn't take her hand; instead, he reached inside his jacket pocket and took out a sealed envelope. "I almost forgot to give this to you," he said as he handed it to her.

"What is this?"

"The salary for the work that has been completed."

She couldn't help but grin—she held in her hand money she had rightfully earned. "Thank you."

"It is I who should be grateful," David said, and finally took her hand in his and bowed over it. Then he brought her hand to his lips and gently kissed it. Her mouth hung open in surprise. She probably resembled a fish, but David continued to smile at her. He released her hand, bowed over Mrs. Patton's hand, and then was gone, taking with him something Lucinda could not name, but missed as soon as he left.

The clock struck ten and David cursed aloud. How could it already be so late in the evening? He'd finished all of his correspondence, approved the contract proposals for Fitzgerald and Grossman, and now all he had left to do was check a stack of ledgers the size of a mountain on his desk.

The ledgers reminded him of Lucinda.

She'd be gone in the morning, traveling to Reading alone. Not that he was worried for her safety. He just didn't want her to go without him. He didn't want to be left out of the end of their adventure. He looked down again at the mountain of ledgers—they weren't going anywhere. But he was.

David pulled on his coat, donned his hat, and left the office.

Fourteen

"**MR. RANDALL, FANCY SEEING YOU HERE** at the train station on this morning of all mornings," Lucinda said archly as David walked up to meet her and Mrs. Patton on the platform.

He yawned. "Shocking, I'm sure, since you are the one who demanded we take the first morning train."

"Come now, Mr. Randall," Lucinda said, tilting her head to one side. "This peevish attitude will not do. You were not even invited."

He opened his mouth to retort and then closed it. She laughed. He ignored her.

David touched his hat to acknowledge Mrs. Patton and then directed a porter to pick up their trunks and his portmanteau. He assisted the ladies into a first-class compartment on the train, then took a seat across the aisle. He tipped his hat over his eyes, crossed his arms on his chest, and pretended to be sleeping, in no mood to make idle conversation with Mrs. Patton.

"I know you are awake, David," Lucinda whispered. "Mrs. Patton has finally fallen asleep."

She must have moved to his side of the aisle, because she nudged him with her elbow.

He didn't respond.

Then he felt a cold finger trace the clean-shaven line of his jaw from his ear to his chin. He jolted up in surprise, and his hat fell to the floor.

Lucinda covered her laugh with her ungloved hand. "I knew you were not asleep."

David was annoyed that his breathing was irregular and that Lucinda's touch affected him so much. "How could I sleep with *you* in the same train compartment?"

"You know I really did not need an escort to Reading," Lucinda said quietly, the teasing smile still lingering on her lips. "I am sure I could have handled myself quite well against any pickpockets or highwaymen we might possibly have met."

"Then you can protect *me*," David whispered as he picked his hat up off the floor and placed it on his head. He slumped back in his seat, his hat covering most of his eyes. But he could still see Lucinda watching him intently. "I know you do not want my protection. I was hoping you'd enjoy my company."

"You do not seem to lack female company."

Did he detect a tone of jealously in her voice?

"I do live with my mother," David said, "and she is an excellent companion."

Lucinda's whole face laughed—her eyes, her cheeks, and her very kissable mouth. He found himself staring at her lips again. She glanced over at Mrs. Patton, who began to stir. Lucinda darted back to her seat on the other side of the compartment. Mrs. Patton blinked and yawned just as Lucinda settled down in her seat.

"What were we talking of again?" Mrs. Patton asked.

"Mr. Randall was speaking of his mother," Lucinda said, and winked at him.

David kept his hat tipped down and rested his head for the remainder of the train ride to Reading. He didn't sleep, but unfortunately neither did Mrs. Patton, so there was no opportunity for conversation with Lucinda without Mrs. Patton's unwanted interjections.

The conductor walked through the aisles between the compartments saying, "Next stop, Reading, ladies and gentlemen! Next stop, Reading!"

David sat up and straightened his hat. Lucinda raised her eyebrows and then gave him one of her light-filled smiles. He returned it.

David assisted both ladies off the train and arranged for their luggage to be brought to a hired carriage. He instructed the driver to take them to the best hotel in the city. The carriage wove through the cobblestone streets and row after row of redbrick buildings, eventually pulling up to a decent-looking hotel on the end of King's Street overlooking the River Kennet. The ladies waited in the carriage while he arranged for three rooms and luncheon.

He returned to the carriage and assisted Mrs. Patton out, then Lucinda. Lucinda's hands were gloved, but he could feel her warmth through them, and he experienced a sudden rush of heat to his body. She brushed her shoulder against his chest and then raised her eyebrows for the second time, as if to proclaim her innocence.

"Do excuse me, Mr. Randall," she said in her mocking voice. "I must have misstepped."

He offered his arm and said gravely, "I should be happy to lend you my arm should you need it, Miss Leavitt."

David half expected her to refuse his help, but she didn't. She linked her arm with his and said, "Thank you, Mr. Randall. I am getting on in years."

"Ancient," he agreed. "Nearly nineteen."

"Past my last prayer."

They followed the proprietor, a Mr. Hart, up the stairs to a small but well-aired private parlor. The proprietor assured them luncheon would be served in half an hour. He then showed them to their rooms. David's was across the hall from the ladies' rooms. Lucinda relinquished her hold on his arm and disappeared behind the dark oak door.

David retired to his chamber to wash up before luncheon. He was happy to remove his hat and shake out his hair. He poured the pitcher of water into the metal basin provided and splashed his face, then ran his wet fingers through his hair in an attempt to put it in some sort of order. Then, he took out his pocket watch and glanced at the time; he still had a quarter of an hour. He walked over to the window and opened it, allowing a slight breeze to enter the room.

He sat in a chair by the window and enjoyed the breeze on his face, leaning his head back and covering his eyes with his arm. It was such a relief to be away from London. Away from his office. His life. His late father's expectations.

David took his arm away from his eyes and picked up his pocket watch. It was nearly time for luncheon. He stood, shook out the wrinkles in his clothes, and left his room for the private parlor. It did not surprise him to see both ladies already there and waiting. He sat at the table next to Lucinda.

"I spoke with a chambermaid and she told me that Burntwood Folly is not more than two miles east of here," Lucinda said brightly. "We should be able to visit the house and return before dinner."

"I should not like to miss dinner," Mrs. Patton said.

David believed her.

Mr. Hart opened the door for several servants carrying cold meats, breads, cheese, and drinks. David was happy to see that his beverage was ale and not milk, like for the ladies. He needed a little stimulant to help him through the afternoon. David watched as Mrs. Patton ate an alarming amount of ham and cold beef, generous helpings of bread slathered with butter, and several pieces of cheese. He could not understand how such a narrow woman managed to consume so much.

Mr. Hart reentered the room. "Is everything to your satisfaction, Mr. Randall?"

"Perfectly, sir."

"I've heard from Bessie that you are planning on visiting Burntwood Folly," Mr. Hart said. "Would you like for me to arrange a carriage for you?"

"That would be most convenient, sir, thank you," David said.

"Do you know why they call it Burntwood Folly, Mr. Hart?" Lucinda piped up.

Mr. Hart looked at Lucinda and gave her a lopsided smile. "Old Mr. Burntwood was rather too ambitious with his architecture, miss. He built half of a grand building and then ran out of funds. And so it sits, half-finished. He tried to call it Burntwood Manor, but folks 'round here referred to it as Burntwood Folly, and it stuck."

The party left a quarter of an hour later. The drive was pleasant, and the first view of the house was rather shocking. It was a large square manor with four tall stone walls, except half of the holes did not possess windows; they were just a shell. It made the other half, although of newer construction, appear to be older. And if David were of a fanciful mind, he would say the entire house looked haunted. Green vines grew up over the stone in the unfinished part of the building.

"Folly, indeed," Lucinda said. "What a perfect setting for a Gothic romance."

"I am sure there is at least one ghost," David said. "Possibly two."

"Two," Lucinda agreed. "You wouldn't want the first ghost to be lonely. There is clearly some nefarious supernatural energy at work, and we have been lured here under false pretenses. Our bodies won't be found for a fortnight or so, and then in the darkest part of these woods. Possibly mangled beyond recognition."

"Lucinda, I do not understand half of what you are saying," Mrs. Patton complained.

David winked at Lucinda, and she gave him her lightest, brightest smile yet. He returned the smile, tightening the link that existed between them.

Once the carriage had pulled up the drive to the front of the house, David helped the ladies out and to the main door, which was painted a bright red. Up close, the disparity between the two halves of the house was even more marked. One side of the house's windows were clean and the shutters painted the same bright red as the door. The other side of the house looked like an abandoned ruin.

The door was answered by a very decorous butler, dressed in an old-fashioned livery and wearing a white wig. He accepted David's card and led the party into a summer sitting room directly adjacent to the main entrance. The dark oak furniture was heavy and out of fashion, but in impeccable condition. Not a speck of dust could be seen in the room.

"I will let Mrs. Burntwood know you have arrived."

They waited for several minutes before an older woman of surprising proportions was wheeled into the room in a chair. Wisps of thin gray hair lay across her large brow; the rest of her hair was covered by a white, lacy cap. She wore a purple dress equal to her size and station. Her jaw was slack, but David could see she had sharp eyes that did not miss any detail of her visitors.

David, Lucinda, and Mrs. Patton stood. David walked toward the startling old lady and said formally, "Mrs. Burntwood, may I introduce myself? I am Mr. Randall, and this is Mrs. Patton and Miss Leavitt. You were so kind as to respond to the letter Miss Leavitt wrote inquiring after the deceased authoress, Mrs. Smith."

The old woman sniffed, her keen eyes catching their every movement. At last she spoke in a gravelly voice. "You are my guests. Please do be seated."

Lucinda sat in the chair closest to where Mrs. Burntwood's wheelchair was placed. David took his seat beside her. Mrs. Patton made herself comfortable on a horsehair sofa.

"What do you fancy folk want to know about Mrs. Smith?"

"Anything," Lucinda said. "Everything."

Mrs. Burntwood laughed, an unsettling sound, almost a cackle. "You're an eager young miss, I'll give you that. Well, the first thing I should tell you is that Bertha was no missus. Never married, and as far as I know, she never even had a suitor."

"Her name was Bertha Smith?" Lucinda clarified.

Her question was met by another cackle.

"Heavens bless me. Bertha's mother were a Smith. Bertha were born simply 'Bertha Topliffe.' I suppose she wrote under Smith for anonymity. Though only the good Lord knows why. You're the first folks to try to track her down."

David could see Lucinda swallow, her face falling. She clearly had been expecting something different. "Mrs. Burntwood, if it is not too impertinent," he inquired, "may I ask in what capacity you knew Miss Topliffe?"

"She were my paid companion," Mrs. Burntwood said. "For more than twenty years. Started off as a governess, but couldn't keep control of the children. She was too apt to be lost in her thoughts. Not ideal for a woman in charge of minding the little ones."

"Did you know that she was an authoress, Mrs. Burntwood?" Lucinda asked.

Mrs. Burntwood nodded and her many chins jiggled. "The publisher demanded fifty pounds to help cover the cost of publishing her first book, *A Tale of Two Towns*. I paid half. And luckily it were a success, and Bertha paid me back every ha'penny. A good girl she was. A good companion."

Lucinda nodded. "May I ask how she died?"

Mrs. Burntwood shook her chins again. "I dunno. The doctor thought it was something wrong on the inside. He bled her a fair bit. I even took her to Bath to drink the waters for several months. But Bertha did not improve. She wasted away to practically nothing, and then she died."

"We are sorry for the loss of your companion," David said empathetically.

"She were a good girl. Very obliging. She'd read to me for hours if I asked her. That's what got her started on novel writing. One day she said, 'I can imagine a better story than this.' 'Write it,' I said, 'Then you can read it to me.' And she did. Listened to my advice on how to improve it too. She were a good girl."

"This question no doubt seems very silly," Lucinda began, glancing at David, "but do you know by chance if she intended Miss Eurydice Emerson to marry Lord Dunstan or Mr. Thisbe?"

Mrs. Burntwood gave another loud cackle. "Can't say I do. She were so sick at the end that she fell behind on getting her chapters to the publisher. I kept telling her that Lord Dunstan was the only one worth considering, but she kept defending Mr. Thisbe. Probably because her brother were a clergyman. She liked all his sanctimony, I suppose. If Bertha ever made up her mind, she never told me. And the last pages she gave me to read, I sent on to her editor."

"Did Miss Topliffe leave behind any other papers or letters, anything that might be of interest?" David asked.

"I sent all her letters and personal papers to her brother, Mr. Elisha Topliffe. He's the rector of St. Ivy's parish."

"How very helpful you have been, Mrs. Burntwood," David said, and looked at Lucinda to see if she wanted to ask anything else. Lucinda shook her head slightly.

Mrs. Burntwood must have seen their unspoken exchange, because she lifted her large hand and said, "You can't be leaving already. I've ordered tea from the kitchen. Now, tell me alls about the exciting life of London society. I am keen to know what goes on nowadays."

David did as he was asked and spent the next half hour sharing society anecdotes with the old woman. Lucinda looked distracted, and Mrs. Patton fell asleep. David was right in his original assessment—Mrs. Burntwood was an intelligent woman. She wanted to know the specifics, as well as the lineage, of every person mentioned. David did his best to satisfy her, and in return Mrs. Burntwood provided him with an array of sweetmeats and biscuits.

At last, David stood. "Mrs. Burntwood, I am afraid we really must leave. But it has been an honor to make your acquaintance, and we deeply appreciate all the information you shared about Miss Topliffe."

Lucinda stood next to him and said in a monotone voice, "Yes, thank you, Mrs. Burntwood. Mrs. Patton, are you ready to depart?"

David watched Mrs. Patton jolt upright as if she'd been awake the whole time. The party took their leave of Mrs. Burntwood and left the house. David assisted the ladies into the carriage, giving Lucinda's hand a small squeeze of encouragement as he did so. Mrs. Patton noticed her pale countenance and suggested Lucinda sit on the same side of the carriage as David.

"We don't want you getting sick, Lucinda," Mrs. Patton said solicitously. "What would your father say?"

Lucinda sat next to David in silence for several minutes, looking out of the window. David memorized the silhouette of her face, then glanced at Mrs. Patton to see if she was still awake. Her eyes were closed, her head slightly forward.

He bumped his elbow into Lucinda's arm. "Are you disappointed?"

She shrugged one shoulder. "I guess I was looking for Eurydice Emerson. Someone young and handsome, with the world at her feet. In control of her own destiny."

"And you found Miss Bertha Topliffe," David said. "Former governess, companion, and spinster."

"It makes me want to discredit everything she wrote," Lucinda said passionately. "What did she know about real life? She lived in such confining circumstances. Her slice of the world was so very narrow, her choices so very few."

"Perhaps she imagined the lives she wished she could have had."

Lucinda seemed to digest this. "Why is it that people are so much more fascinating in fiction than they are in real life?"

"I disagree," David said, and gave her his cockiest smile. "No one in print is half as fascinating as me."

"I shan't agree, because it would only pamper your vanity," Lucinda said.

"You haven't *dis*agreed."

"If only we were alone," Lucinda began, eyeing Mrs. Patton across the seat.

"Lucinda, you are making me blush," David whispered.

"I wasn't—I didn't say—You should not tease me, David," Lucinda managed at last. "I am having a very disappointing day."

David moved his knee to touch hers, briefly. "I know," he said. "I was simply trying to cheer you up."

Lucinda pressed her knee against his and nodded. She let out a loud sigh, and David could see her thoughts spinning behind her eyes. At last, she said, "I do not understand why Mrs. Burntwood did not simply write in the letter for us to inquire after Mr. Elisha Topliffe, of St. Ivy's rectory."

"That's simple enough," David said. "The old lady wanted a visit."

"From complete strangers?"

"I've found that some people, whatever their age or sex, need company," David said thoughtfully. "She was a lonely old lady who wanted visitors, and in return she gave us information in our search for your authoress."

"I am so disheartened," Lucinda said. "I am not sure if I wish to continue."

"That is a pity," David said. "I suppose I will have to visit Mr. Topliffe all by myself. Without yours, nor Mrs. Patton's, most excellent company."

Lucinda gave him a reluctant smile.

"You've changed a lot since we were children, but you

haven't changed that much," David said in a tone so low that Lucinda had to lean closer to him to hear. "And the Lucinda I know will not be content with an unfinished story. Even if she doesn't like the ending, she will want to know it all the same."

"Are we discussing Miss Topliffe's story or Miss Emerson's?" Lucinda asked.

"I believe they are one in the same."

Fifteen

THE LANGUOR THAT ACCOMPANIED THE visit to Burntwood Folly clung to Lucinda all the way back to the hotel in Reading. She barely touched her dinner and claimed a headache afterward, excusing herself to her room. She did not undress, nor did she lie in her bed, but rather paced back and forth from the door to the window. From the window to the bed. From the bed to the door. Circling her cell over and over.

Silently, Lucinda cursed the restraints put on women by society. What real choices had Bertha Topliffe had? She was wellborn enough, but without money. Her options in life were few: become a governess, a companion, or a wife. Nothing else was genteel enough for the daughter of a gentleman. Yet

Bertha had dared to dream of more. She'd written novels and found a publisher, only to die from an unknown internal complaint. And even at the time of her death, she had still been the companion of an old lady. Had Bertha ever truly escaped the lot into which she was born?

Lucinda was not the daughter of a gentleman, but she had the advantage of money. And money meant more now socially than it ever had before. But, if anything, her options were even fewer than Bertha's. Her only option was to marry, preferably to someone of good birth and social standing.

It simply was not fair.

If she had been born a boy, she could have had her choice of vocations. She could have traveled on the train without a companion. Even walked down the street by herself. Such a simple luxury she would never experience.

Lucinda had let herself believe that discovering the end to Eurydice's story would somehow complete her, would complete that chapter of her life from finishing school where the only ray of hope was a few pages of story in a monthly magazine. She thought it would allow her to continue on to the expectations of her new life. But she felt unfinished, like the story. Finishing school had taught Lucinda how she was supposed to behave and what she was allowed to think, but both her heart and her mind rebelled against their rigid rules. Their demeaning dictates.

How could she ever be a complete person if she couldn't be her true self?

Lucinda heard a light knock at her door. She paced back to it and opened it. David stood in the hall. He pressed a finger to his lips and then whispered, "Would you care to go on a walk with me?"

"Yes," Lucinda whispered back. "Why are we whispering?"

David pointed to Mrs. Patton's room, and Lucinda instantly understood. She reentered her room and picked up her bonnet. She tied it haphazardly underneath her chin. She ought to have grabbed a shawl, but it was already so hot outside, and she didn't want to add any more clothing to her body than what was already there.

Lucinda followed David out of the hotel. He stopped outside the front door. He looked at her so closely that she felt her temperature rise.

"What?" she asked.

"Your bonnet," he said finally. "Might I retie it for you? You look rather lopsided."

Lucinda stuck out her chin in response. David deftly untied the knot and repositioned the bonnet on her hair, then meticulously tied the bow underneath her chin on the left side. Lucinda had not realized she was holding her breath until the moment he let go of her ribbon. She slowly exhaled, feeling the delightful tension between them. He offered his arm, and she did not hesitate to take it.

The sun was setting in the distance, giving the buildings and surrounding green fields a golden glow. They walked down the street next to the River Kennet, and Lucinda found the sound of water calming. They continued to stroll down the cobbled street until they saw where a part of the river split off into a small canal. One side was diverted north toward ruins; the other side of the river continued its path east.

"Shall we keep to our path or go see some specters in those ruins?" David asked.

"Definitely the specters," Lucinda said. "I wonder what that building once was? It looks like it might have been a castle."

"I do not know," David said, leading her down a narrow street toward the ruins.

The path ended abruptly, so they turned west for a few steps before heading north down another short street. On one side there was a building that looked as if it had partially collapsed; there were wooden trusses supporting the structure. It appeared to Lucinda as if the building were being rebuilt from the outside in.

"Whatever happened here?" she exclaimed.

To Lucinda's surprise, it was not David but another gentleman who answered her. "Abbey Gateway collapsed in a gale earlier this year, ma'am."

Lucinda saw a man walking out of the structure. He had a substantial brown beard and wore a pair of narrow spectacles and the clothes of a gentleman.

"Sir," David said, bowing his head. "I am Mr. Randall. And you are?"

"Sir George Gilbert Scott," he said, doffing his hat to Lucinda. "I'm the architect in charge of restoring Abbey Gateway to its original glory."

"So, those ruins over there were part of an abbey?" Lucinda asked.

"The abbey's chapter house, commissioned by Henry I, it was, nearly seven hundred years ago," Sir George explained.

"Of great antiquity, then," David responded.

"And historical significance," Sir George said, puffing his chest out a little. "This here gateway that I'm restoring was used as a schoolroom, and the famous Miss Austen attended school here with her sister."

"That is fascinating," Lucinda said. "I adore Miss Austen's works. *Emma* is my favorite."

"The Reading Corporation also recently acquired the Forbury and created the gardens just there," Sir George said, pointing his stubby finger directly northeast of the ruins. "It's certainly worth a visit."

"Then we shall visit it," David said. "Thank you for your information, Sir George."

They continued to stroll arm in arm. They left the road and took a gravel footpath toward the great stone ruins, following a dilapidated rock wall that must have connected originally to the abbey. They entered the main building underneath a stone arch. It looked to have once been at least two stories high. There was no sign of any roof, and some of the remaining stone walls were higher than other parts. Light streamed through arched openings that once must have been windows, and green plants were growing right out of the thick stone walls.

"I wish to amend my earlier statement," David said.

"Yes?" Lucinda prompted.

"This is a much more promising site for ghosts than Burntwood Folly."

Lucinda laughed, the sound echoing off the crumbling walls. "This location certainly has an atmosphere to it. Look, through that arch, I see the Forbury Gardens that Sir George mentioned. Shall we go explore them before it gets too dark?"

"Lead on, Lucinda."

They walked down another gravel footpath to the gardens, which had a lovely fountain bubbling water from the top with four spokes of walking paths surrounding it. Formal flower beds in long rectangles and perfect circles were full of bright yellow, red, white, and pink blooms, and they passed exotic trees of several varieties that Lucinda could not name.

"It's beautiful," she breathed.

David gave the gardens a critical look. "It's rather too well kept for me."

"You'd prefer something overgrown."

David turned to look her in the eyes. "Yes, overgrown with a nice big thornbush to push you into."

Lucinda laughed. "That is not very gallant of you, David."

"I need an excuse to be near you," he said.

Lucinda removed her arm from the crook of his elbow and

turned so she stood directly facing him, so close she could feel his warm breath on her cheek.

"I am near now."

David put his hands on her shoulders and pulled her toward him, closing the small space between them, and gently placed his lips on hers. Once. Twice. And then a third time. Just lightly, like a soft breeze.

Then he looked at her, their noses nearly touching, a silly grin on his face. Lucinda was quite sure the expression on her face was equally sappy, but she couldn't help herself. She had never felt this way before. She'd never been kissed before. It was as if her insides were a bubbling fountain of happiness in the garden of her heart.

A twig snapped, and Lucinda pulled away from him. David blinked at her in surprise, and she inclined her head toward a pair of men walking through the park. He nodded ever so slightly.

"It is getting dark," he said. "Should we head back to the hotel, Lucinda?"

He did not offer his arm, but his hand. Lucinda placed hers inside it and interlaced their fingers. He gave her another of his ridiculously handsome smiles. The happiness in his face made her heart beat irregularly. They did not say much on the walk back to the hotel, but Lucinda thought what they had shared did not require mundane words.

Lucinda could not seem to wipe the sappy grin off her face the next morning. Not even during the dull train ride home, when Mrs. Patton persistently spoke about her noble relations and David pretended to sleep again. He "woke up" when the train arrived in London and escorted them home. Mr. Ruffles took their hats and wraps and stood waiting to open the front door for David.

"Thank you, Mr. Randall, for your escort," Mrs. Patton said. "We poor females would have been quite lost without it."

He took her proffered hand and bowed over it. "A pleasure, ma'am."

"One moment, Mr. Randall," Lucinda said quickly as he turned to leave. "*My father* left some papers for you."

Mrs. Patton was already on the first stair, but turned as if she was going to follow them.

"Go unpack, dear Mrs. Patton," Lucinda said. "My father's business with Mr. Randall will not take me more than a minute."

She yawned. "Very well, but see that Mr. Ruffles accompanies you. You cannot be alone with Mr. Randall."

"Perish the thought," Lucinda said. She saw David turn his head away to conceal his smile.

She walked down the hall to the sitting room and waited for Mr. Ruffles to open the door for herself and David. Before Mr. Ruffles could come in, she took the doorknob handle and said, "That will be all, Ruffles. Thank you." She thought she saw the solemn butler smile a little as she shut him out of the room.

Lucinda turned and found herself in David's arms. She stifled a giggle.

"What shocking behavior, Mr. Randall," Lucinda said, pretending to be affronted. "What if a servant were to walk in?"

"You're right," he said. "What a scandal that would be."

Lucinda cupped his face and kissed it lightly before stepping away from him. They were not close enough to touch, but stood a foot apart, smiling foolishly at each other.

"Thank you for coming with us, David," Lucinda said. "I enjoyed your companionship."

"Just my companionship?" David asked, his eyebrows raised.

Lucinda folded her arms across her chest and shook her head slightly. "A lady never kisses and tells."

"Learned that at finishing school, did you?"

"You'd be surprised some of the things I learned in finishing school."

"I look forward to being enlightened," he said, and Lucinda felt deliciously breathless. "Although I have a great deal of work to do."

"I hope the papers I have been reviewing have lightened your load."

"So very much," David said. "You are much quicker with the figures than I will ever be."

Lucinda swallowed a lump in her throat. "I was thinking . . . that possibly . . . perhaps . . . you could speak to my father about allowing me to work at the office."

David didn't reply, but she knew he had heard her.

"Will you speak to my father on my behalf?"

"I do not think it is my place to interfere," David said after a long pause.

"But you are his business partner," Lucinda said.

"He is your father," David replied. "It's a family matter, not a business matter."

Lucinda stepped back from him. "I thought you were my friend, David."

"I am your friend," David insisted, trying to move closer to her. He held out his hand, but she resolutely folded her arms. "But legally your father has the right to decide whether or not you are allowed to work."

"I know! That is why I need your help persuading him. Tell him of all the work I have already done. Show him that I am capable. Treat me like your equal!"

David shook his head slightly, and Lucinda felt anger flash through her entire body.

"I am sorry, Lucinda. I can't risk it."

"What is the risk?" Lucinda asked, louder than she meant to. She clenched her hands into fists to stop them from shaking in her folded arms.

"A permanent rift between myself and my partner, to start," David said, gesticulating with his hands. "The ramifications to the company are countless. We could lose contracts. Connections. Stocks and speculations. So much of the business is based on our united reputation."

Lucinda could stand still no longer. She unfolded her arms and paced back and forth, breathing heavily, unable to release the anger and frustration that coursed through her.

"Lucinda," David said, touching her arm. "Lucinda, please listen to me—"

She brushed off his hand. "I think I have done quite enough of that today, Mr. Randall."

"I'm just—"

"More worried about the business than you are about me. And I was foolish enough to think that you were different. That you saw me as an equal. But you want to keep me in a decorated cage just like every other man I've ever met. To be petted and admired like a pretty, brainless bird!" And then she said the worst possible thing she could think of. "David, you're a pigeon-livered fopdoodle!"

His immediate reaction was everything she had hoped for. His eyes widened in shock and his jaw clenched. But then he laughed, loudly. The anger in Lucinda boiled over to fury. She had just spoken the most offensive thing in her entire life and he was *laughing* at her?

"Stop laughing! It is not funny!" Lucinda nearly yelled.

"I am sorry, Lucinda. I did not mean to laugh, but you caught me off guard," he said, still smirking. "Your father uses the same phrase frequently."

"And do you laugh when he says it?"

"Of course not."

"I thought not. Women cannot even curse, it seems,"

Lucinda said. She walked resolutely to the door and opened it. Mr. Ruffles was standing in the hall outside, and he'd probably overheard their entire conversation. "Mr. Ruffles, would you please see Mr. Randall out?"

"Lucinda—" David was at her side, looking at her imploringly, all trace of amusement gone.

"*Now,* Mr. Ruffles," Lucinda said, and left the room without glancing back at him.

Sixteen

DAVID PULLED THE BRASS KEY to his house out of his pocket. He looked up and down the street before inserting the key into the lock and turning it, relieved not to see anyone he knew. He felt deflated, like a pillow with all of the feathers pulled out of it. If only Lucinda would have let him explain himself. If only he hadn't laughed. He hadn't meant to, but her words had shocked him and, he had to admit, amused him. He couldn't picture Miss Clara Hardin, or even the American Merritt girls, calling him a pigeon-livered fopdoodle. Lucinda was one of a kind, and he'd gone and ruined everything.

He walked into his house and set his portmanteau on the marble-tiled floor of his foyer, locking the door behind him.

"David, there you are," his mother said.

He turned, and his mother walked toward him with her hands outstretched. David took her much smaller hands in his own and gave his mother a kiss on the cheek. She released his hands, but continued to stand close to him, examining his face.

"You look so tired, dear."

"Do I?" David said, taking off his hat and setting it on top of the portmanteau. "I've been traveling, Mother. Stayed the night in Reading. I am sorry I was not home when you arrived. I didn't know when to expect you."

"The housekeeper said we missed each other by mere hours," his mother said. "Come with me to my sitting room. We have much to catch up on."

"I really do not have the time—" David began, but stopped midsentence when he saw the look on his mother's face. It wasn't anger, or sadness. It was disappointment—keen disappointment. She had often worn that face when his father had been alive. "I would be happy to come, Mother. My business can wait another hour."

His mother gave him a small smile, but the disappointed look remained on her face. He followed her down the hall to the private parlor reserved for her particular use. It was a small room, with only a sofa and a couple chairs. The windows faced the small garden behind the house. David took his seat beside his mother on the sofa.

"What do you wish to tell me?" he asked.

His mother took his hand in both of hers. "You are very good to me, dearest. And I do not mean to complain, but I so rarely see you these days or nights."

"You've been at Keynsham Hall."

"Before then, David," his mother said. "It seems that every hour of your day and most of the night is spent at your countinghouse."

"It's been busy lately."

She frowned at him. "For more than a year now, you have missed social engagements. I have attended most of the parties without you as my escort."

"I am sorry, Mother."

She shook her head. "I do not mean to complain of neglect, or to imply that I need your support. In fact, this conversation is not about me at all. It is about you."

"Me?"

"Dearest David, you work so much that I fear you have no life of your own outside of the business. You've lost track of all your friends from Eton. You no longer hunt or fish. I could barely drag you for three days to the country for your aunt's house party. You are not your father. You do not have to live like he did."

David stood, forcing his mother to release his hand. He walked to the window and looked out at the flowers in the small garden. "I am very good at business. Better than Father ever was."

"I do not doubt it."

"I have more than doubled our investment in the funds, as well as invested in the consols. Mr. Leavitt says I have a shrewd eye for which speculation will be the most profitable."

He heard his mother sigh. "The money was never enough for your father either."

"It isn't about the money."

"What is it about then, David?" she implored. "Your father?"

"My father is dead."

His mother stood and walked toward him. "But I see his influence over you every day. You do not need to prove yourself to a dead man. A man who could never see you for the incredible person that you are."

"He wanted me to be more like Francis," David whispered.

A tear fell down his mother's cheek. "Francis is dead. Your father is dead. And you, my dear son, are all I have left. And you seem to have no life at all outside of work."

"My work is important," David said. "It gives us our place in society."

"But as your mother, I want you to have so much more in your life than work," she said. "That is why I have encouraged you to find a wife. Why I asked your aunt to invite Miss Hardin to Keynsham. I was hoping you would spend more time at home if you had agreeable company. That it would give you something else to focus your time and efforts on."

"I have other interests besides the business."

"And what would they be?"

David desperately tried to think of a hobby he could use to defend himself. "I have literary pursuits," he blurted out. "I've been assisting Miss Leavitt in her search for the family of the deceased authoress, Mrs. Smith, and the true ending of her unfinished story."

"Did Miss Leavitt also stay in Reading?"

"Yes," David said, and exhaled slowly. "Why have you never called on her?"

His mother clasped her hands and shrugged her small shoulders. "I visited her mother only once. Her breeding . . . She was not our kind of person. I did not visit Miss Leavitt for the same reason. She is not of our same class."

"And yet you were civil to her at Keynsham Hall."

"I am not a gorgon, David," his mother replied. "And I am not blind. I saw that you are fond of Miss Leavitt, and I am very fond of *you*."

"Will you call on her?" David asked.

"Yes," his mother said. "If you promise me that you'll call on one of your old friends from Eton."

A laugh tore from David's throat, though he felt anything but humorous at the moment. "You know how to drive a hard bargain, Mother. Perhaps you should have taken over Father's share of the business," he said. "Very well, I promise I'll visit Charles Noble next week. Now, I really must attend to some business today. It cannot be delayed."

"Very well," his mother said. "But don't forget, we are pledged to the Warrens tonight for dinner."

"I will be there," David said, and left the private parlor.

It was already seven o'clock in the evening when David left his house dressed in his black dinner clothes. He told his coachman, Evans, to drive him to the Warrens' house on Hay's Lane. He tapped his cane against his shoe with impatience; he was supposed to be there by now, and with each minute he was later. It was just a dinner party, for goodness sake, not a parliamentary debate. But he could see the disappointment on his mother's face already.

And Lucinda. He didn't want to think about her, but he couldn't stop thinking about her.

David opened his leather bag and reviewed the leases from the bank. It was still light enough to see every word of the first lease on a second warehouse near Chamberlain's Wharf. He was reading the addendums when the carriage rolled to a halt.

"Why are we stopped, Evans?" David called, irritated by the further delay.

"Mr. Randall, sir, look out your window!"

David lifted his eyes from the papers he had been reading. "Good heavens!"

The light in the carriage was not from the setting sun, but from red and orange flames that engulfed Hay's Wharf and Chamberlain's Wharf. Even the River Thames was ablaze. The monstrous fire continued in all directions, its apocalyptic destruction devouring everything in its path. And it was headed toward Tooley Street. To his office. His official documents. Everything he had worked so hard on would be consumed.

David dropped the lease. He opened the carriage door and got out, knocking off his hat in the process.

"Evans, take the horse and carriage a safe distance away," David commanded, and began to run toward Tooley Street.

Lucinda seethed as she added the numbers in the column.

How could he? How dare he? Why wouldn't he help me?

David's response was that it was a family matter. But the few times she saw her father, he rarely allowed her a word, let alone a proper argument. Well, she wasn't a little girl anymore. And she wasn't going let her father dismiss her like a child. If he refused to speak to her at home, she would go to his office with or without his permission.

She stood resolutely, the crinoline cage underneath her dress shifting as she moved. She refused to be caged any longer. Not by her clothing. Not by her father. Not by her sex. And certainly not by society's expectations.

She strode out of the morning room and out the front door of her house. Hatless. Without her shawl. Without a chaperone. Nothing but the clothes she wore and the coins in her reticule. She hailed a hackney coach and told the driver to take her to Tooley Street.

Lucinda twiddled her thumbs as she watched the familiar streets pass. The carriage stopped two blocks away from the countinghouse. Lucinda poked her head out of the hackney coach to see the driver and ask why they had stopped.

"Can't go no farther, ma'am," the driver said. "Fire ahead."

Lucinda handed the driver a couple of farthings before stepping down out of the coach.

"Thank you, sir," she said, and began to run toward Tooley Street.

She heard him call after her, "Stop, miss, it ain't safe!"

Lucinda kept running, pushing past all the people fleeing the fire. It wasn't until she reached Tooley Street that she saw the enormous flames engulfing the warehouse district by the River Thames. Fire was spreading in all directions.

Lucinda thought quickly as she caught her breath. Her father would still be in his office. All the other clerks would have gone home at five o'clock. They would be safe. But he would be working with his back to the window, not wanting to be distracted by the outside world.

She clutched at her side, cursing both her corset and skirts, and continued to run toward the office. The front door was locked. She pushed against the door with her shoulder, but it did not budge. She looked around frantically, until finally she saw a loose cobblestone in the street. She dropped to her knees and pried it up. With all of her might, she used it to hit the glass window over and over again until there was a hole big enough for her to crawl through. She cut her hand on the ledge and fell forward as her large skirt caught on the glass.

Lucinda stood up, bruised and scraped and her hand bleeding. She painfully hobbled down the hall and up the stairs to her father's office. When she opened the door, she found him slumped over in his chair. Orange flames danced higher and higher behind the closed windowpane.

"Father!" she screamed.

But he did not move. Lucinda grabbed his wrist—she could feel his weak pulse. Lifting his arm over her shoulder, she began to drag him slowly from the office. They had not yet reached the door when the window shattered behind them, the flames beginning to eat into the room. Black smoke filled the air, and Lucinda could hardly breathe. She closed her mouth as tightly as she could and with both arms pulled her father's body down the hall to the stairs. She lifted him up with the last of her strength to carry him down, but her foot caught in the crinoline cage and they both fell down the stairs.

Everything was black.

People of all classes were gathered in the streets and on the bridges, watching the great fire as if it were some sort of spectacle. David's pace slowed to a walk. There were simply too many people, all pushing forward for a better look. This did not stop him; David used his size to make his way through the crowd. He felt his shoulders and back pushed by countless unknown hands and fingers.

As he got closer, David could see members of the London Fire Establishment and several privately owned fire engines attempting to fight the blaze from the warehouses with their water hoses. Even two blocks away, David could feel the heat of the flames, which reached higher than thirty feet in the air. He breathed in the black smoke, covering his ears as explosions erupted from the burning warehouses. The air smelled of burned tallow and oil.

David continued to press his way through the crowd, bumping and inching forward until he reached the top of Tooley Street. He grabbed his handkerchief out of his coat pocket and covered his mouth and nose. The air was thick with smoke, and he was beginning to find it difficult to breathe. And although he knew that street well, it was hard to see. He felt a hand on his shoulder.

"You, sir, get back to safety!" a burly constable yelled in David's ear. He shoved David back where he came from, his grimy hand covered in black soot. "I'm to keep this street clear for the fire brigade."

"I am Randall of Randall and Leavitt, and that is my countinghouse," David said, pointing down the street. "I have important documents there that cannot be replaced. I will only take what is essential. I won't be long."

"You can ask Fire Engineer Tozer; he's in charge of this street," the constable said. "I'm not to let anyone pass, sir."

The constable marched him back to the end of Tooley Street. David covered his mouth and nose with his handkerchief again, the smoke like a thick, dark fog. The constable pointed to a man near the closest fire engine.

"That's Fire Engineer Tozer. You can ask him."

David jogged the thirty feet between him and the fire engine. Half of the fire brigade were still pointing hoses at the impossible flames. The other half were receiving drams of spirits from an older man with white hair, who David assumed was Tozer. He strode up to him.

"Fire Engineer Tozer, I need you to instruct the constable over there to allow me down Tooley Street," David said. "It is imperative that I visit my countinghouse."

"I'm not Tozer," the man said. As he came closer, David could smell brandy.

"Then please point me to him," David said impatiently.

"I am Superintendent James Braidwood," he said, "and trust me, I would not be doing my job if I let any soul go down that street until this flame is contained. If we don't contain it, Tooley Street will be ashes and so will you. Now you go about your business and I will go about mine."

Before David could protest, Superintendent Braidwood carried his jug of brandy to a group of men from the fire brigade standing by the wall of a warehouse behind Tooley Street. David could see the superintendent giving instructions. *I could have been back by now,* David thought. He walked two steps toward Braidwood when another explosion pierced his eardrums. The acrid smell of saltpeter filled the already smoke-filled air. David fell down to the pavement from the force of the blast.

Lucinda rubbed her eyes and cried out as her injured hand touched her face. She could see—barely. The room was full of black smoke and flames were on the stairs. It was hotter than a furnace. Her father's body was draped awkwardly over her legs. They had to get out. Time was running out for both of them.

Lucinda attempted to stand, but fell back to her knees, coughing and sputtering. She put her arms underneath her father's shoulders and scooted backward toward the door, no longer able to see through all the smoke.

Her back bumped the wall. Lucinda managed to stand and felt her way to the door. She did not have the strength to lift herself or her father through the window. She found the doorknob and cried out when she touched it with her injured hand, the metal so hot it burned her hand through her tattered gloves. She grabbed a fistful of her skirt and finally managed to turn the knob, falling through the door as it opened.

Lucinda took a few deep breaths of the cleaner outside air before crawling back on her hands and feet for her father. His body was illuminated by orange flames, and she could feel the fire's heat as she used the last mite of her strength to drag her father to the door.

She sat on the street to catch her breath, but she could still feel the heat. Lucinda looked down and saw her skirt was on fire. She grabbed the unaffected part of her skirt and tried to smother the flames, but they continued to climb from her ankles all the way to her knees. The fire burned her hands. It was her blasted crinoline! The steel framework was making it impossible for her to extinguish the flames by covering them.

She had to get to her feet. Struggling to stand, she pulled desperately at the ties of her skirt—now fully ablaze. Wrenching herself free of the crinoline cage and skirt, she pulled off her smoldering blouse and collapsed on the street next to her father.

David got back to his feet just as the wall of the warehouse crumbled before his eyes. Bricks rained down on Braidwood and the five other men from the fire brigade. David stepped back in shock. The firemen were completely buried, and the monstrous fire had leapt on to the buildings of Tooley Street. The orange light was so bright, it could have been midday.

"This way!" a round man with a large mustache yelled. The fire engines moved past David on both sides and stopped just short of where the men were buried in the rubble. The round man passed David and gave him a shove. "I'm Fire Engineer Tozer, and I am now in charge. And you can get out of the way!"

"Are you going to save them?" David asked.

"No," he said, and he looked down. "There isn't time. The fire's spreading too fast. Now, sir, get out of the way!"

David stepped back. The man he had talked to just five minutes before was dead or dying underneath a pile of bricks. Even the most important business papers in the world were not worth his life. He turned to go.

"Help!"

At first, David thought the voice belonged to one of the men in the rubble. But it was too high-pitched for that. It was a woman's voice.

David recognized that voice.

His heart froze inside his chest.

Lucinda.

She must have gone to the office to speak to her father because he had refused to help her. Refused for his own selfish reasons and personal insecurities.

Panic at the thought of losing her flashed through his veins. There were so many things he wanted to unsay.

David pushed past the constable, running down the street into the flames and smoke.

"*Lucinda!*"

Lucinda tried to get up, but she did not have the strength. She tried to roll over, but the pain in her arms and hands was too excruciating. Her entire body revolted against her will. She closed her eyes. She did not want to die here and now on this street, leaving so much of her life unfinished.

"Help," she rasped, and then coughed and coughed.

"Help!" she cried again as loudly as she could.

She thought she heard someone respond in the distance.

Lucinda closed her eyes. She could do no more.

Moments later, she felt someone wrap a cloth around her. And strong arms lifted her up underneath her shoulders and legs.

"My father," she muttered, without opening her eyes.

"The firefighters have him," a man's voice said. It sounded remarkably familiar. "Just hold on, Lucinda. Just hold on."

She tried to nod, but everything went black again.

David froze in horror when he finally reached the counting-house.

Lucinda, lying in the street. Covered in soot and wearing nothing but her corset and smallclothes. Surrounded by flames.

He tore off his jacket and wrapped it around her before scooping her up in his arms. He felt blood as her hand brushed his. His only coherent thought was to get her away from the fire, to get her to safety.

In that moment, he knew that he loved her. More than his business. More than his father's expectations. More than his very life.

But she was so hot in his arms. It was like she was on fire.

She murmured something, asking about her father.

"The firefighters have him," he assured her, struggling to keep his voice calm.

She seemed to relax a little at that.

"Just hold on, Lucinda. Just hold on," he asked her.

Begged her.

Directed by the constable, two men from the fire brigade carried Mr. Leavitt away from the fire. Away from the ashes of their countinghouse. They placed him on the ground near where the constables were holding back the crowds who had come to watch the spectacle. Then the firefighters returned to their posts, trying to contain the fire as acre upon acre of London burned.

David knew he had to get Lucinda and her father to a doctor. But there were people everywhere. Carriages and omnibuses were caught in the middle of the street, unable to move. He couldn't carry them both, and he couldn't leave one behind. Not the woman he loved, nor the man who was like a father to him. It was an impossible choice.

David held Lucinda tighter to his chest, breathing heavily. Onlookers pressed in closer to them, and he heard a few whistles and several exclamations.

He saw a burly man dressed in the clothes of a tanner standing in the front row of the crowd. David stumbled toward him. "Please, help me. I can pay."

The tanner nodded, and two of the constables let him through their blockade. At David's direction, the tanner lifted Leavitt as if he weighed no more than a paperweight.

David resolutely walked toward the crowd, and the people shifted to let him and the tanner through. David could feel thousands of eyes on them. On Lucinda's beautiful form—burned, bruised . . . and inadequately concealed by his dinner jacket. But he couldn't think. He had to keep his feet moving.

The press of the crowd lessened. Eventually, the air no longer burned his lungs with each ragged breath. His burden became easier. He could see again.

As he came within a block of the Leavitts' house, David focused on each footfall. Left and then right. Left and then right. With the last of his strength, he climbed the front steps and kicked the door.

The door opened quickly; clearly Lucinda's absence had not gone unmissed.

David recognized the butler and Mrs. Patton, followed by an older woman who was dressed like a housekeeper with a white apron and lace cap.

"Good gracious!" Mrs. Patton shrieked, covering her mouth with a handkerchief. For a moment, David thought she was going to faint.

"Get a hold of yourself, Mrs. Patton, this is no time for hysterics," the housekeeper said in a loud voice. "Mr. Forbes, come here at once."

A footman ran toward them, pulling on his livery jacket, and bowed to the housekeeper.

"You and Mr. Ruffles will carry Miss Leavitt inside and to her room. Then go and fetch Doctor Clayson."

"Yes, ma'am," the footman said.

"I'll take her shoulders," the butler said in a choked voice, "and, Forbes, you take her feet. Carefully now."

David didn't want to let Lucinda go.

"Rest, sir," Mr. Ruffles said gently. "She's safe now. We'll take good care of her."

The two men carefully lifted Lucinda from his stiff, tired arms and carried her into the house and up the stairs.

The housekeeper's loud voice rang in his ears. "Mrs. Patton, make yourself useful. Go and tell the cook to start preparing bandages and Nancy to bring fresh water upstairs."

Mrs. Patton blinked and lowered her handkerchief from her mouth, and turned to walk farther into the house.

The housekeeper pointed to the tanner and said in a quieter tone, "Please, sir, would you be so good as to bring Mr. Leavitt this way?" The tanner followed the housekeeper inside.

David's legs would no longer hold him. He sank heavily onto the front steps.

Several minutes later, the tanner left the house, closing the front door behind him. David dug at his pocket for some coins.

"No, no," the man said. "I didna do it for the money. God bless ye and them two."

David watched the tanner walk away down the street until he could no longer see him.

Then he buried his face in his hands and sobbed.

Seventeen

NEVER-ENDING DARK.

And a voice calling from a great distance.

Just hold on, Lucinda. Just hold on.

It was David's voice, she was sure now. But she was so very tired, and in so much pain. She longed to give herself over to the safety and quiet of the darkness. But his voice kept calling her back. Begging her to stay with him. She wanted to, for David. She cared for him after all, even if she was still furious with him. But she was so very, very hot. She was burning up from the inside and turning to ash.

Lucinda opened her eyes cautiously. The sunlight of the room burned them, and she blinked several times. The pain lessened each time she opened her eyes, until she saw the figure of a man sitting in the chair beside her bed. Through the blur, she saw he wore a black suit, but she couldn't see his face.

It must be David, she thought, and her heart beat faster.

She tried to speak, but her mouth was so dry. She tried again and managed to say only one word. "Water."

The man stood. "Yes, Lucy, I will see that you get water."

Lucinda's thoughts were clouded, but that voice did not belong to David. It was someone else's. Someone she knew. Lucinda tried to sit up, but her whole body constricted with pain. Her arms hurt. Her legs were bruised and stiff from falling down the stairs. Her head felt tender as it fell back onto the pillow. The pain overwhelmed her, and she lost consciousness.

She roused again when a glass was pressed against her sore, chapped lips. A gentle hand was behind her head.

"Just a few more sips, Lucinda," the voice said.

It was a lady's voice—Mrs. Patton's.

Lucinda blinked, willing her eyes to focus on the face above hers. She could see the sharp profile of Mrs. Patton's chin, but not the finer details. The older woman took the glass of water away and in its place put a small bottle to Lucinda's sore lips.

"A little more, Lucinda," Mrs. Patton said. "And you will be off to sleep again."

Lucinda gulped and nearly choked on the liquid in her mouth but managed to swallow the draught. It tasted bitter. She opened her mouth to ask what the liquid was, but before she could speak, her eyes became too heavy to hold open. Her mouth went slack. The pain that had overwhelmed her moments before slipped away into a blurry haze of nothingness.

When Lucinda opened her eyes, her room was dark. She blinked several times. Was she blind? She opened her eyes wider and noticed the shadows in the room. It was only nighttime. She exhaled in relief. Then Lucinda heard a light snore. She turned her head to look at the chair and found a figure sitting in it. She could not make out the details of the person, but Lucinda knew that snore.

"Water. Please," Lucinda asked Mrs. Patton.

She heard Mrs. Patton yawn and then the clicking of the gas lamp as she turned it on. The light made Lucinda's eyes hurt, so she closed them, but repeated her request. "Water. Please."

She heard Mrs. Patton stand and felt the woman's gentle hand behind her head.

"Open your mouth, Lucinda," she said in a singsong voice, as if she were talking to a small child.

Lucinda obeyed and felt the welcome relief of liquid flowing into her dry mouth and throat. Mrs. Patton removed the glass from Lucinda's lips.

"More," Lucinda breathed.

"Of course, dear girl," Mrs. Patton said, "but only a little at a time. Too much and you will be sick again."

Lucinda did not remember being sick, only falling down an endless hole of nightmares. Over and over again, like riding a wooden horse on the horrible carousel at the fair. Spinning around in circles but never going anywhere, forced to repeat the pain and the grief of her darkest moments forever . . . being beaten with the strap at finishing school . . . her mother's death.

Mrs. Patton picked up the little bottle from the table and placed it at Lucinda's lips. But Lucinda bit her lip and shook her head. "No."

"It's laudanum, Lucinda," Mrs. Patton explained in the same patronizing voice. "The doctor prescribed it for your pain."

Lucinda shook her head even harder, starting to give herself a headache. "Water."

Mrs. Patton placed the vial back on the bedside table and lifted the glass once more. Lucinda drank greedily. When at last she was satiated, she pulled her head back. "Thank you."

Mrs. Patton placed the glass back on the bedside table.

"I want my mother."

"I am sorry, dear girl," Mrs. Patton said, "but your mother is dead."

Lucinda shook her head again. "I know. She's been dead for ten years. I want my mother's portrait in my room."

Mrs. Patton frowned in confusion. "There is no portrait of your mother hanging in this house."

"I know," Lucinda said through clenched teeth. "But there used to be one over the fireplace in the sitting room of our previous house. My father had it taken down. I don't know where it is. Most likely the attic. But I want it. And I want it now. Ask the housekeeper."

"I promise to look into your request first thing in the morning," Mrs. Patton said. "Now, just take a few drops of laudanum and you will sleep like a baby."

Lucinda growled. "No laudanum. I'd rather the pain than the nightmares. And I don't care that it is the middle of the night. I want my mother's portrait *now*."

Mrs. Patton nodded and carried her gas lamp out of the room. Lucinda lay in darkness for several minutes. Possibly an hour. The pain increased in her burning hands and arms with each moment, but Lucinda did not change her mind. She did not want any more laudanum. She closed her eyes. Maybe Mrs. Patton would not come back until the morning.

Then Lucinda heard the scuffling of footsteps, more than one pair of feet. The door opened, and the light of the gas lamp filled the room, stinging her eyes. Mrs. Patton carried the lamp into the room, followed by two male servants carrying a large parcel. They were followed by the housekeeper, Mrs. Wheeler, in her nightdress with a shawl around her shoulders. Lucinda held her breath as the servants untied the hemp string and unwrapped the portrait from the paper.

"Where do you want it, Miss Leavitt?" Mrs. Wheeler asked.

"By me," Lucinda whispered. "I want my mother by me."

Mrs. Wheeler placed a chair next to Lucinda's bed and bid the servants to place the portrait on it. She carefully straightened the portrait, angling it so Lucinda could see it from her bed. Lucinda opened her stinging eyes further, so she could see her mother's brown eyes and her bright smile. Even through the blur, the face was shockingly like her own. As if she were looking through a mirror darkly.

Eighteen

DAVID CLOSED HIS EYES AND leaned his head back against the carriage seat, but the image of Lucinda, burned and bleeding, would not leave his mind. Forcing him to relive that horrible day over and over again.

He pressed a handkerchief to his nose and mouth. The ringing in his ears was not from the explosions, but from church bells. It sounded like every church in London was playing the funeral peal in honor of Superintendent James Braidwood's procession. David rode in his cousin's carriage behind the Duke of Sutherland and the Earl of Caithness, as the chief mourners. He glanced out the carriage window. All the shops were closed on the street. Rows and rows of bodies flocked to watch the funeral procession. He saw the members of the crowd take off their hats and bonnets as the hearse passed by.

David could almost feel the press of the crowd against him in the carriage. The way they had surrounded and touched him when he'd carried Lucinda the night of the fire. He swallowed.

"Are you all right, David?" Alfred asked from the seat adjacent to him.

David wiped his forehead with his handkerchief and replaced it in his pocket. "Only hot," he said.

"Nearly a week later and they say the fire is still burning," Alfred said. "But at least it is contained."

"It may be a fortnight or more before I can see what is left of my countinghouse," David said.

"Have you lost a great deal of money?" his cousin asked.

David shook his head. "It is impossible to say. The building itself was insured. But all the documents burned. Every contract will be in question. Every lease renegotiated. Our solicitors will probably be very busy for the next year, at least."

Alfred pulled a paper out of his pocket and handed it to David. It was a bank draft for one hundred thousand pounds from the Bank of England.

"What is this?"

"All of the amount owing with interest on Keynsham Hall's mortgages," Alfred explained. "Mr. Merritt thought you might need extra funds after the fire to rebuild your business. Maybe buy an estate of your own."

"How?" was all that David could manage to say.

"It's a part of the marriage settlements."

"Whose marriage settlements?"

"Mine," Alfred said with his catlike smile. "Miss Persephone Merritt has done me the honor of accepting my offer of marriage. But her father wants the estate free and clear of debt first."

"Are you sure?" David asked.

Alfred pushed David's fingers over the paper. "Yes, David. You no longer have to carry my burdens. I will soon have a wife for that."

"And how is Miss Merritt?"

"Happy, I hope," Alfred said. "We are to be married in less than two months."

"I hope you will be happy too," David said.

"I shall do my poor best."

"You're not poor anymore."

Alfred gave him a crooked smile. "My rich best, then."

David stood on the front step of the Leavitts' house and knocked on the door. His mind could not help but cast back to the last time he had stood here, with Lucinda in his arms. The butler opened the door and quietly ushered him into the sitting room, only this time Lucinda was not in the room brightening up everything around her. He walked over to the table to set down his leather bag, when he saw the papers that he had forgotten to take with him after their disagreement.

"Good heavens!" he exclaimed, picking up the three separate stacks of papers and riffling through them. Leases. Deeds. Ledgers. David's most important documents had not burned in the fire after all—they had been safely here in the Leavitts' sitting room.

Relief and regret swept over him. Sweet relief that details of the Durham speculation were safe, each paper signifying thousands of pounds of his hard work. But he felt bitter regret that he had nearly risked his life for a few signatures that had not even been at his countinghouse to begin with. He carefully placed the papers inside his leather bag.

"Mr. Randall," Mrs. Patton said from the doorway. "To what do we owe the pleasure of this call?"

David took off his hat and held it in both hands. "Mrs. Patton, I was hoping for news of Miss Leavitt. How is she doing? Is she any better?"

Mrs. Patton came into the room and closed the door behind her. "I am delighted to tell you the doctor believes that Lucinda will live. Although she is scarred."

"May I see her?"

Mrs. Patton shook her head. "I am afraid that would be most improper, Mr. Randall. Lucinda is confined to her bed, and as her chaperone, I could not allow an unrelated gentleman into her bedroom."

"But you would be there the entire time, Mrs. Patton," David said. "Surely there can be no scandal in a short, chaperoned visit to an invalid confined to their bed?"

"I suppose so, if it is a very short visit," Mrs. Patton said doubtfully.

"I promise you, I will not stay more than a few minutes," David said. "I must see her."

Mrs. Patton gave a resigned sigh. "Follow me."

David did not have to be told twice. He grabbed his leather bag before trailing behind her. They walked up the stairs to a room at the end of the hall where Lucinda was asleep. Her dark hair swirled out in wild curls around her face on the white pillow. Her skin was deathly pale, and her lips were chapped. He could see bandages on her neck, hands, and arms. He walked closer to her and stood beside her bed.

"Lucinda, you have a visitor," Mrs. Patton said in her singsong voice from the bottom of the bed.

Lucinda's eyes flickered open and widened when she recognized him. David smiled down at her and their eyes met—his heart swelled with renewed hope. But then she closed her eyes and turned her head away from him without saying a word.

"I-I brought you a new book," he said, and pulled the slim leather volume out of his bag and placed it on her bedside table.

Lucinda still didn't look at him.

"It's called *Silas Marner* and it's by George Eliot, but Mr. Gibbs assures me that it was actually written by a lady named Mary Ann Evans," David explained. "I thought you might enjoy it."

But there was still no response from her. David could

almost believe she had fallen back asleep; her eyes were closed and she didn't move a muscle.

"Mr. Randall," Mrs. Patton said, as she briefly touched his arm. "I think you'd better go."

David nodded. "Goodbye, Lucinda."

With a sinking heart, he followed Mrs. Patton down the flight of stairs and to the front door.

"Should I come back again tomorrow?" he asked.

"She needs time to heal, Mr. Randall," Mrs. Patton said in a sympathetic voice. "The best thing you can do for Lucinda is leave her alone."

David did not trust himself to reply. He simply nodded and left the house. His carriage was waiting for him, and he instructed his driver to take him to his warehouse.

Randall and Leavitt's warehouse was on the other side of the fire, on the opposite bank of the River Thames. He had previously regretted that their warehouse was such a distance from the countinghouse, and now their separation was the only reason his business was still operating. He watched out the window of his carriage as it bumped over London Bridge.

Smoke and sparks of fire were still actively burning around what once had been Tooley Street. Men, women, and children were wading neck-deep into the Thames, trying to salvage any of the goods that had been expelled there by the explosions. David coughed several times and then covered his mouth and nose. The usual smog of London blended with the smoke was a lethal combination.

His carriage stopped in front of his warehouse. He thanked Evans and carried the documents inside the building. David had set up a temporary countinghouse in the west corner of the warehouse, where his clerks were working diligently to replace the lost information from the fire. He climbed up the stairs to a small landing that overlooked the entire warehouse, into what was formerly the foreman's office, and was surprised to see Mr. Leavitt sitting at the desk. His gray hair was going in all directions, and he had a long, red scratch on the left side of his face above his beard. He flipped through the papers on his desk with a manic frenzy.

"It's not here. They're not here," he kept repeating over and over. "Not here. Nowhere."

"Sir," David said. Mr. Leavitt looked up, his eyes red and unfocused. "Should you be here, sir?"

"I must work. I must work. Work is the only thing I can do," Leavitt said, and began again to riffle through the papers.

"You should be with your daughter."

Leavitt shook his head, not looking up. "Just like her mother. I couldn't protect her. Just like her mother."

David walked over to Mr. Leavitt and grabbed one of his shaking hands. "What are you looking for, sir? Perhaps I can assist you."

Mr. Leavitt yanked his hand out of David's grasp. "The Durham pages. Must find the Durham pages. Gone up in flames. Everything I hold dear, gone up in flames."

"I have the pages."

"What?" Leavitt wiped his sweaty brow and seemed to regain some control over himself. "What a relief, Randall. But how?"

"Your daughter has been helping me with my work for over a month now," David said slowly. "And she is exceptionally talented with numbers. She is the reason these papers are not in cinders, and all she wishes is to be given a chance in this business. She would be the perfect choice, nay, the *only* choice, for our chief financial officer."

"She's burned. Lucy is burned," Mr. Leavitt said, running his hands through his wild hair.

"Lucinda will be all right," David said. "And you should be at home with her. Not here. Not working. Durham can wait."

Mr. Leavitt took a long, shaky breath, then nodded. "Durham can wait," he echoed.

David took his mentor by the arm and helped him to his feet, then handed him his hat and his cane. It was as if Mr. Leavitt had aged twenty years in the fire.

David helped him out of the warehouse, hailed a hansom cab, and escorted him home to the care of the butler. Then, David climbed back into the hansom cab, and instead of instructing the driver to return him to his office, he called out, "Paddington Station."

"Very good, sir," the driver said.

When they arrived, David paid the driver, then purchased a ticket for the next train and got on it. He sat in a first-class compartment all by himself, grateful for the solitude. He opened the window and let the fresh air in, closing his eyes.

It was impossible not to think of Lucinda. His last few train rides had been in her company. He longed to see her. To hold her close to him. To kiss her. To make her laugh and to see her smile of pure light. But could their relationship ever be the same again? Would she ever forgive him?

He buried his face in his hands. If only he had heard her call for help sooner. If only he had agreed to talk to her father. Then she would not have gone to Tooley Street that night. She would be unharmed, but his mentor and partner would have burned to death. David understood choices and consequences from business. Everything had a cost. Nothing was free. And sometimes you did not realize how great the cost was until you had already paid it. Or the true value of something you possessed until you lost it.

David got off the train at the next stop and began to walk. He just wanted to get away from people.

He needed to think.

To breathe clean air.

To be alone.

Once he was clear of the town, he took off his hat, his coat, and his waistcoat. He undid his cravat and unbuttoned the top two buttons of his shirt. The air felt good against his bare skin. He walked down the pike road for a mile or so, when he heard the sound of running water. He left the path and trudged through the dusty field until he found a small river winding its way through the trees.

David took off his boots and waded knee-deep into the stream. For the first time since the fire, he didn't feel hot. He put his hands into the water and splashed his face. He laughed. He stomped through the water as if he were a boy again. Free from responsibilities, from his father's expectations. Free to enjoy himself. He eventually waded back to the shore and lay underneath a tree, balling up his coat for a pillow.

It seemed that his work was taking over every minute of his life. He put his arm over his eyes, blocking all light. David enjoyed the business, and he relished the status he received for being a part owner in such a successful venture. He wanted to prove to himself, and to his dead father, that he was every bit as shrewd a businessman as his father had been. But when would it be enough? After the Durham deal? Another year? Another decade? An entire life spent trying to show a dead man that he was capable?

David wanted to be more than his father, more than just a successful businessman. He wanted to be an acquaintance. A friend. To actually have time to visit his club, see his old cronies from Eton. Play a game of cricket. Join a fox hunt. Maybe purchase his own house in the country and stay for long weekends. Accompany Lucinda to find other lost authors. He could not imagine a future without her in it. Her laughter, her witty remarks, and her very kissable lips.

Nineteen

LUCINDA BROUGHT HER HAND TO her mouth and tried to chew on her thumbnail, only to taste cotton. She spat out the little bit she'd bitten off and exhaled loudly. Her nose began to itch, and no matter how she tried, she could not scratch it with her bandaged hands. She couldn't do anything!

She heard the scuffling of footsteps and closed her eyes tightly. She was in no mood for another conversation with Mrs. Patton. Lucinda heard the doorknob turn and two distinctly different footfalls.

"Oh, dear, Miss Leavitt is sleeping," Mrs. Patton said. "Shall I tell her you called?"

"No," Persephone said with her thick American accent. "I shall sit here until she wakes up."

"Very well," Mrs. Patton said. "I shall go order you some tea, then. Shall I?"

"Please."

Lucinda heard Mrs. Patton leave the room and close the door behind her with a click.

"You can open your eyes, Lucinda," Persephone said. "I can tell you are not asleep. Your breathing is not regular enough for sleep."

Lucinda opened her eyes and smiled at her friend. Persephone gave her a brilliant smile in return. "I am here to get you back on your feet."

"I haven't walked yet," Lucinda said, gesturing to her legs beneath the coverlet. "My arms were badly burned by the fire."

"Then your legs should work just fine," Persephone replied, helping Lucinda sit up. "You need to get your strength back quickly so you can be one of my attendants at my wedding."

"What wedding?" Lucinda exclaimed. "You're getting married?"

"Yes, dear, that's what wedding means."

"To Lord Adlington?"

"No, to the Archbishop of Canterbury," Persephone said with a laugh. "Of course I'm marrying Alfred."

Lucinda laughed for the first time since the fire. "I am so delighted for you both."

"Excellent. I'll have my dressmaker come next week and take your measurements."

Lucinda covered her face with her bandaged hands. "I can't be your attendant, Persephone. Not how I look now."

Persephone gently pulled each of Lucinda's hands from her face and looked her squarely in the eye. "You are still one of the most beautiful women I have ever seen."

Lucinda shook her head. "I'm bruised and broken."

Persephone stamped her foot and put her hands on her narrow waist. "You are not a doll. You are a woman. And women don't break that easily."

"I was ridiculed by society when I was lowborn and beautiful, and now I am lowborn and scarred," Lucinda said. "There is no place in society for me now."

Persephone harrumphed and grabbed a hand mirror from the side table. She held it in front of Lucinda's face. "Look. I see a pair of perfectly lovely blue eyes, a dainty nose Miss Clara Hardin would kill for, and rosy lips."

"I see a bruised face, hair that has been singed off, and pink spots of discoloration on my neck from where I was burned. I see hands that will probably never play the pianoforte again, and I may never even be able to hold a pen."

Persephone handed Lucinda the mirror. "Let's start with the hair, then."

She walked around the room opening drawers until she found a brush and returned to the bed. Persephone gently took off Lucinda's nightcap and slowly began to brush her hair, starting at the bottom and working her way to the roots. Persephone gave Lucinda's hair one last comb-through before placing the brush on the bedside table.

"Sit tight, Lucinda," she said. "I shall be back in a jiffy."

What is a jiffy?

A jiffy was not a long time. Persephone returned to Lucinda's room with a pair of brass scissors. "Hold still while I cut off the burned bits."

Lucinda sat still, watching chunks of her hair fall onto her coverlet. She picked up her mirror and gasped. Her hair was short and uneven.

"Put that mirror down until I am finished," Persephone bade her.

Lucinda set the mirror in her lap and closed her eyes. She felt the cool, sharp edge of the scissors brush against her neck.

"There now," Persephone said, picking up the mirror and holding it so Lucinda could see. Lucinda gingerly touched the short curls around her head. The haircut was certainly not the prevailing style, but it framed her face and accentuated her high cheekbones. Lucinda shook her head and felt the light, easy movement of her hair.

"You're supposed to compliment me now on my excellent haircutting skills," Persephone said with her usual smile.

"Thank you," Lucinda managed. "I like it."

"Good," Persephone said, placing both the scissors and the mirror on the side table. "Next, we must get you dressed."

"I don't want to—" Lucinda began to protest, but Persephone was not listening.

She opened Lucinda's wardrobe and selected a tartan day dress with bright reds, greens, and blues. She laid the dress on the bed and adjured Lucinda to lift her arms. Lucinda took off her nightdress and felt the welcome relief of air on the upper part of her exposed arms. Her forearms were carefully wrapped in bandages.

"Where shall I find a corset and a crinoline cage?"

"I will never be caged again," Lucinda said stubbornly. "That blasted contraption nearly burned me alive."

"No crinoline, and I'm sure you don't need a corset to fit into your dresses," Persephone said. "You've lost at least a dozen pounds these last weeks. And no wonder with what you've been through! Let's just slide this dress over your head. Don't worry, I will be gentle."

And Persephone was as she inched the dress over Lucinda's bandaged arms and gingerly buttoned the back of it. Lucinda carefully shifted her legs off the bed. They felt bruised and stiff, swollen from disuse. Persephone gently pulled two stockings onto Lucinda's legs and placed two slippers on her feet.

"A brilliant lady's maid was lost in me," Persephone teased.

"I am sure you will enjoy being a countess much more."

"You're right, I shall," Persephone said. "Put this arm around my neck."

Lucinda did as she was told. Persephone placed her other arm around Lucinda's back and together they stood up. Daggers of pain shot up Lucinda's legs, and she gasped. Her friend steadied her.

"The first step is always the most difficult," Persephone assured her.

Lucinda bit her lip and nodded. She lifted one of her sore feet and placed it a few inches in front of the other.

"You are a strong woman," Persephone said.

"I am a strong woman," Lucinda repeated as she took her next agonizing step.

"You can accomplish this task."

"I can accomplish this task."

"You can accomplish any task."

"I can accomplish any task," Lucinda said in a breathless voice. "I can accomplish any task."

Persephone helped Lucinda walk a turn around the room before assisting her back into her bed. She swept the hair off the coverlet and onto the floor as Lucinda leaned back against her pillows. Her legs felt afire again, but at least she could feel them. And without her crinoline cage on, she could see her legs too.

"Yes, rest up," Persephone said. "We shall walk again in an hour."

Before Lucinda could protest, Mrs. Patton returned with a tea tray. She blinked several times. "Lucinda," she said in a shocked tone, "you are awake and dressed."

Persephone stood and took the tea tray from Mrs. Patton's hands. "Thank you for the tea, Mrs. Patton. Why don't you get some rest and I will watch Lucinda for a few hours? I am sure you are exhausted from this last week."

Persephone placed the tea tray on the table and gently guided Mrs. Patton out of the room, closing the door firmly behind her. She wiped her hand over her brow. "Whew! I thought she was going to stay, and I'm sure she will not approve at all of what we are going to talk about."

"What are we going to talk about?" Lucinda asked in surprise.

"Have you ever heard of bloomers?"

"*Bloomers?*"

"Mrs. Amelia Bloomer is an American who advocates reform in women's dress," Persephone explained. "She wears pantaloons, which are just like men's trousers, but looser and come in at the ankle with lacy fringe."

"She doesn't wear a skirt?"

"No, she does wear a skirt over the pantaloons," Persephone said as she handed Lucinda a cup of tea. "But the skirt is much shorter and barely past her knees."

"Did she start a scandal?"

"Yes!" Persephone said excitedly, placing her own cup of tea back on the table with a clatter. "And lots of New York society ridiculed her and the other women who followed her in dress reform. They nicknamed her pantaloons 'bloomers,' but she wears them anyway. She does not seem to care what others think, and neither should you."

"I wish I didn't care what others think," Lucinda admitted, "but I do."

"Well then, I suppose pantaloons are not for you after all," Persephone said.

"You think I should wear bloomers?"

"I thought you no longer wished to be caged."

"I don't."

"Then stop caring what other people think. That's the greatest cage of all," Persephone said. "The only person's opinion that matters is your own. And mine. Of course."

"Of course," Lucinda said, accepting a plate laden with more food than she had eaten in a week. "Aren't you going to help me? My hands are bandaged."

"You'll never get better until you start to learn how to do things for yourself again," Persephone said, laughing wickedly as she added, "or you'll starve."

Lucinda pushed the biscuit off the plate with her bandaged hand and onto her skirt. She pushed it a bit more before she was able to pick it up and take a bite. "You are a wretched nurse."

"You are a wretched patient."

"I don't know how to thank you enough—" Lucinda began.

"Silly Lucinda. This is what friends do," Persephone said, taking a large bite out of a biscuit.

Lucinda looked at herself in the mirror without a stitch of clothing on. It had been over a month since the fire, and she no longer needed to wear her bandages. Her arms showed dark pink blots of discoloration where she'd been burned. The backs of her hands were roughened with countless scars. She turned over her hands and looked at her palms. On her left hand, she could see branded into her palm the grapevine decoration from the doorknob of her father's office. Oddly enough, the doctor said this burn might have saved her hand; it had cauterized the cut from when she fell through the window. She moved each stiff finger one at a time. It still hurt, but it was getting easier.

The two angry, reddish-pink blots on her neck had faded, and the doctor told her that in time they could fade further. Or they could remain the same.

I am a strong woman.

I can accomplish this task.

I can accomplish any task.

Lucinda pulled on her shift, ignoring the pain of moving her arms. She put on her undergarments, then stepped into her pantaloons and tied them at her waist. She pulled the shortened dress over her head and sighed in satisfaction. She had dressed herself. Mostly. Nearly covering all of her scars.

She pulled the cord for a servant and saw *Silas Marner,* the book David had brought her, sitting on the table. She carefully picked it up in her scarred hands. She couldn't turn the pages yet, but Mrs. Patton had kindly read it to her while she was recovering. *Silas Marner* was followed by *East and West,* and finally *She Knew She Was Right*.

"Don't you want to know which suitor Eurydice picked?" Lucinda had asked her when Mrs. Patton read the last published words.

"Anyone can see that Eurydice would have picked Lord

Dunstan. She was practically penniless, and he was wealthy with a title," Mrs. Patton stated as if it were fact.

"But you don't know for sure. Eurydice never showed a decided preference for either suitor," Lucinda had pressed. "Won't you please write to Bertha Topliffe's brother, the rector of St. Ivy's parish, and ask about her final papers? I would do so myself if I could hold a pen."

Mrs. Patton had shaken her head resolutely. "There is no need to waste the good rector's time over a silly little thing like a fictional novel." And once Mrs. Patton's mind had been made up, there was no persuading her otherwise. She even told Lucinda it was unladylike to persist in asking her.

Lucinda turned over the book in her hands, feeling a pang of regret. David had not come back to see her since the day he brought *Silas Marner* and she'd refused to look at or speak to him. She'd been embarrassed by her appearance, and she was still angry at him for refusing to help her. But she thought he'd come back. And the more she recovered, the more she wanted him to come and see her. But he hadn't.

The servant opened the door, and Lucinda set down the book. Her maid buttoned Lucinda's dress and helped her put on stockings and slippers. Then, she carefully arranged the front curls of Lucinda's hair and hid the rest of the short curls underneath a lacy snood.

Lucinda heard a knock at her door.

"Come in," she said.

Mrs. Patton entered the room. Her disapproval of Lucinda's

clothing choices was apparent from the thin line of her mouth. "Your father is waiting to speak with you, as you requested. He is in the sitting room."

Lucinda stood gingerly, letting her skin ease into a different position. She pulled on her gloves, thanked the servant and Mrs. Patton, then bowed and left the room. She held the banister lightly as she slowly navigated the stairway. Lucinda stopped when she reached the bottom of the stairs, took several deep breaths before continuing down the hall to the sitting room, and then another as she opened the door.

Her father was standing at the windows with his back to her, but he turned as he heard Lucinda approach. Like Mrs. Patton, his eyebrows lifted as he took in her pantaloons.

"It's an American fashion Miss Merritt told me about," Lucinda explained. "A reform movement in women's dress to make it more practical, yet still pretty."

"It is interesting," her father managed.

Lucinda sat on the settee and looked up at her father. She could see his discomfort in the stiff way he held his shoulders and turned his head.

"I have wanted to talk to you, Father, for some time," Lucinda began. "In fact, the reason I was in Tooley Street during the fire was so I could say something that I have wanted to say for many years."

Her father blanched at the mention of the fire. "My poor Lucy. I wish I had burned to ash instead of the pain and anguish you have suffered and will continue to suffer."

"I knew the risk when I saved you," Lucinda said. "And I am not a child anymore, and I do not wish to be treated as one."

"You are a young woman."

"I am a human being," Lucinda countered. "With a knowledge of numbers and mathematics that few possess. And as heir to your share of the business, I wish to be a part of it. To use my skills."

"I sent you to finishing school to rid you of this nonsense," he said, still standing above her. Looking down at her.

Lucinda stood and looked down at him. "You sent me away from everything I knew and loved, to people who despised me for my birth."

"Everything I have done," her father said, "I have done for your good."

"No, you have done it for yourself!" Lucinda cried, and then added in a quieter tone, "Because you never took the time to ask me what *I* wanted. What I want now."

"Lucinda, you can't fight the way of the world."

"The world is changing," Lucinda said.

"It has not changed that much."

"And it never will change until brave people stand up for what they want and fight against foolish rules that have no reason behind them."

"If you were a man—"

"It was not a man who saved you from a burning building," Lucinda said, pressing a scarred hand to her breast. "It was me. Your daughter."

Her father slumped down into a chair. Lucinda sighed loudly and sat down again on the settee.

"If you were to work at the office," her father began, "you would lose all opportunity to find a suitor from a good family. To be included in a society that your mother and I could never dream of."

"My mother," Lucinda said, unable to stop the tears from falling from her eyes. "Why did you take her from me?"

"She died."

"You obliterated her from our existence. You removed everything that reminded me of her from our home, and then you made us move," Lucinda said.

"The reminders were too painful."

"She was my mother," Lucinda said slowly. "I deserve to know who she was and where she came from."

"There isn't much I can tell you," her father said, shaking his head.

"Then tell me what you know."

Her father looked down at his hands and didn't speak for over a minute.

"She was born in Lisburn, Ireland, but she didn't like to talk about her life there," he said at last. "Her family had been spinners and stockingers for centuries, but their handloom products could not compete with the new water-powered loom machinery. They lost almost everything before her parents sold their home in Lisburn and immigrated to England. Her parents died of typhus soon after arriving. Your mother tried to find work in London, but she was despised for her poverty and for being Irish. She was finally lucky enough to obtain work as a nursery maid, where she worked long hours for little pay and no respect or appreciation from her employers. Did you want me to tell you that? Jane would not have wanted you to remember her that way."

"I don't even know her maiden name," Lucinda said.

"Johnston. Jane Johnston," he said. "She liked alliterative names. That's why she named you Lucy—Lucinda Leavitt. She loved you so much. She wanted you to fit into English society like she never could. Like I never could."

"You could be a part of that society," Lucinda countered. "You could come with me to Miss Merritt and Lord Adlington's wedding. And if a suitor does not approve of my working in a countinghouse, I would not want him."

Her father covered his bearded face with his hands and then ran them through his gray hair. "You are stubborn, like your mother was."

"I am *strong*, like my mother was."

Her father heaved a large breath. "If working at the office is what you truly want, then I will not stand in your way any longer. Randall told me he thought you'd make a fine chief financial officer, and I believe he's right."

Lucinda's chest felt suddenly tight. David hadn't forgotten her. He'd even talked to her father about her working for the business.

She stood again. Not quickly. She couldn't stand quickly. She walked over to her father, put her arms around him, and kissed the top of his bald head. He flinched, and Lucinda released him and stepped back.

"I love you, Papa," she said.

He stood and patted her on the head. "I love you too, Lucy."

Twenty

DAVID STRAIGHTENED THE LAPELS OF his jacket and walked down the steps of his cousin's house. He was nearly at the bottom of the stairs when he heard a slight groan. He turned to see Lucinda standing at the top of the stairs. She was dressed in an outlandish fashion—a shortened dress, baggy pantaloons that tightened at her ankles, and a contraption that covered most of her hair in a white net, leaving only her front curls exposed.

She barely touched the railing with a gloved hand. She made a slow step down. And then another. He could tell each step pained her, but it didn't stop her. David regained his senses and ran up the stairs by twos until he was close enough to touch her. But he didn't. He just stared at her in tongue-tied wonder. He wanted to tell her so many things but was unable to come up with even one coherent sentence.

So he took her into his arms and hugged her close, never wanting to let go of her again.

Lucinda carefully returned his embrace, moving slowly to not aggravate her healing injuries. They stood there, wrapped in each other's arms for what felt like an eternity and yet not enough time at all.

Then, David wordlessly scooped her into his arms and began to carry her down the stairs. She smelled of roses, and her dark curls tickled his chin.

"I can walk," she said, settling her arms around his neck. "I don't need any assistance. I burned my hands, not my feet."

"I know," David said, clutching her closer to him.

"Then why did you pick me up?"

"Because I wanted to."

Lucinda laughed and looked up at him. "When did you arrive?"

"Late last night," David said. "Took the last train. Had a few tasks I needed to accomplish before coming today."

"Business, no doubt," Lucinda said. "I hope you did not bring any business papers to the wedding."

"Only one," David said, grinning at her. "I will show it to you later, if you'd like."

David reached the bottom of the stairs, but he did not put Lucinda down. Nor did he continue toward the breakfast room. Instead, he made a sharp right and carried her down a corridor toward a small private parlor that had been his grandmother's favorite room.

"You can put me down now," Lucinda said.

"Are you sure?" he asked. "This is a rather pleasant arrangement, after all."

"Extremely pleasant," Lucinda agreed, biting her lip to hide a smile. After a few moments, she asked, "Where are you taking me?"

"A place where we can talk."

"Are we not talking now?"

David placed a light kiss on Lucinda's head. He was delighted to see her blush.

"Oh, that kind of talk!"

"Precisely."

David gently set Lucinda on her feet and opened the door to the private parlor. The room was no longer used, so all the furniture was covered and the curtains drawn. David closed the door behind them and walked to the windows to open the curtains. He yanked them back, releasing a swarm of dust mites into the air. He looked over his shoulder at Lucinda. She pulled off the sheet covering the sofa and sat.

"Perhaps we should do both types of talking," she suggested.

David nodded and took a seat beside her. He reached for her gloved hand. "May I hold this?"

"Yes, please," Lucinda replied, placing her hand in his.

"I have missed you more than I can possibly express."

Lucinda wrinkled her nose. "Then why didn't you come visit me again after you left *Silas Marner*?"

"I thought you didn't want me to. I thought you were still angry with me. You wouldn't even look at me," he said. "And Mrs. Patton told me you needed time to heal."

To his surprise, Lucinda laughed. "Poor Mrs. Patton. What a trial I was to her. I do hope her new charge will be more to her taste."

"Your father dismissed her?"

"She resigned when she saw my pantaloons, and Father gave her a generous bank draft as a goodbye," Lucinda said. "Had I known adopting reform dress would rid me of the woman, I would have adopted it sooner. Do you like them?" She lightly kicked her feet forward to show them off.

"I like *you*," David replied.

"I am not the same as I was, David," Lucinda said. She swallowed. "We can forget about our light flirtation and remain friends, I sincerely hope."

David lifted her hand to his lips and kissed it. "You may not be the same, Lucinda. But my feelings have not altered."

Lucinda pulled her hands from David's and took off each of her gloves, showing him her scars. David took off his own gloves and gently took her hands into his. Softly, he ran his thumb over the brand of the doorknob, and then placed the gentlest of kisses into her palm. Then he took her other hand and did the same.

"I may never hold a pen again," Lucinda said. "My hands may never regain their former mobility."

"I am not in love with your hands."

"Love?" Lucinda asked breathlessly.

"Love," David repeated, then cupped her face with his hands. "I love you more than I had ever dreamed was possible. I realized how much you meant to me when you were surrounded by flames. I knew then there was nothing I would not do for you. I spoke to your father on your behalf—"

Lucinda pressed a finger to his lips. "I know. He told me—chief financial officer. It has a nice ring to it."

David kissed her finger that was on his lips. She smiled at him, her smile that lit up the room.

"You are supposed to say something," David whispered, his lips nearly brushing hers.

"My mother was an Irish immigrant," Lucinda said, watching him closely for his response.

David blinked. "And that is why my mother didn't visit your mother or you."

"I did not know until after the fire," Lucinda explained. "I demanded my father tell me about her. Her name was Jane Johnston. She was an Irish orphan, the daughter of spinners who made stockings and gloves. And I resemble her greatly. So much that my father has difficulty looking at me."

David caressed her hand softly with his thumb and said at last, "She must have been very beautiful if she looked like you."

"She was so very beautiful," Lucinda said. She paused before asking, "Do you mind that I am not . . . that my origins are quite common?"

"You are anything but common. You are rare, for I have never met anyone else like you," David said. "And that is why I love you. And you were going to say . . ."

"Words are always inadequate," Lucinda whispered, pressing her lips to his.

David returned the kiss, softly exploring her mouth with his own. He moved his lips down to the line of her jaw and made a row of kisses. He saw two pink blemishes on her neck that had not been there before. He softly pressed his lips to each one.

"Words are inadequate," David said as he kissed her just below her ear. "But I am a businessman. I need to hear every word. Every particular."

He felt her roughened hands gently graze his cheeks and run through his hair. She stood slowly and then sat on his lap.

"Is this seat taken, sir?"

David only grinned in response and put his arms around her waist, pulling her closer.

Lucinda put her arms around his neck and whispered in his ear, "Mr. David Randall, I love you. I love your every particular. From the hairs on your head to your toes that I look forward to treading on for the rest of my life."

And then she kissed his ear, his cheek, and his lips. It

was like no other kiss. This kiss was as hot as fire and burned him from the inside. He gently pulled the net off her dark curls and explored her silken hair as they continued to add kiss upon kiss until at last breaking off for breath. Lucinda tucked her head underneath his chin, and he cradled her against him.

She pulled her head away from his chest and pressed her hand against his coat pocket. David heard the rumple of paper.

"What is this?"

David pulled the thrice-folded paper out of his pocket and unfolded it. Lucinda's eyes widened in surprise. "You purchased Wincombe Park from Mrs. Smith?"

"You said you liked it," David reminded her.

Lucinda laughed. "I did."

"Perhaps you and your father would be willing to visit me there?"

"Perhaps," she said, and kissed him on the nose. "If you plant a row of thornbushes."

"I'll plant an entire garden of them."

David and Alfred stood in the vestibule of St. Mary's Church waiting for the rector. It was a medieval building, the brick masonry a patchwork of colors. A large stained glass window gave most of the light to the building, depicting St. Mary with an enormous halo encircling her hair. Alfred began to pace back and forth. Back and forth.

"Where is the blasted rector?" Alfred asked.

David heard the unmistakable sound of vomiting outside the door. "I believe he is indisposed."

Alfred hit his fist against the stone wall of the church. And then cursed as he shook out his hand. "The wretched man is sick today, of all days."

"This is why you have groomsmen," David said calmly. "Tell me in which direction I will find the closest rector and I will return with him as fast as I can."

"There's a small village not two miles away," Alfred said. "Follow the south pike road and you can't miss it."

David clapped his cousin on the shoulder and strode quickly out of the church. He climbed into his cousin's carriage and directed the driver where to go and to get there as quickly as possible. The driver took him at his word, driving at such a pace that the carriage shook and David felt rather ill. He covered his mouth with his gloved hand, breathing in and out slowly. Alfred didn't need two people in the marriage party sick today.

The carriage stopped in front of a small rectory adjacent to a village church. David hopped out and dashed up the steps to knock on the door. A serving girl answered, her doe-like eyes widening when she saw David in his silk cravat and elegant wedding clothes.

"Is the rector here?"

"This way, sir," she said, giving him a quick bow.

She led him from the small entry to an office. She knocked

on the door before opening it. "A gentleman to see you, Rector."

David entered the room and saw a small man, roughly somewhere between fifty and sixty years of age, with an abundance of white hair and thick bushy sideburns connected to a mustache, but a clean-shaven chin. He stood when he saw David.

"Now, what can I help you with today, sir?"

"I am Mr. Randall; my cousin is Lord Adlington, the Earl of Adlington," David explained quickly. "He is getting married today, but the rector of St. Mary's is suffering from a stomach complaint and is unable to perform the ceremony."

"And you wish for me to take his place?"

"Please, Rector," David said and then added, "Immediately."

"Give me a minute to get my coat, hat, and holy robes. I will be with you in a trice," the rector said, giving David a reassuring smile. "Don't worry, Mr. Randall. They will not start without us."

David nodded.

The rector returned in less than two minutes, wearing his coat and his hat and carrying his robes in a box. He accompanied David into the carriage, and the driver departed with all haste.

The rector interweaved his fingers on top of his box, seemingly unperturbed by the carriage's careening progress. "Perhaps you can fill me in on a few details before we arrive."

"I would be happy to."

"You have already told me that the groom is Lord Adlington," the rector said, "but what is his full name?"

"Lord Alfred Peregrine Daniel Randall, fifth Earl of Adlington."

"Very good," the rector said. "And the young lady's name?"

"Miss Persephone Merritt."

"Merritt?" the rector said, as if he were trying to place the name.

"American," David clarified.

"Ah," the rector said, folding his arms.

David noticed a black armband around his arm, indicating the rector was mourning someone.

The rector must have noticed where David was looking, because he said, "My sister died a few months ago."

"I am sorry."

"Our lives in this world are so fleeting," the rector philosophized. "But special moments like today make life worth living."

David agreed warmly, though he was not thinking of his cousin's wedding, but rather of Lucinda.

The carriage stopped, and David gestured for the rector to leave first. The rector left the carriage and, without a glance back at David, entered the side of the church. The next time David saw the man, he was fully dressed in his holy robes, standing at the front of the chapel next to Alfred. They were illuminated with color as they stood underneath the stained-glass window. David walked up to the front of the church and took his place at Alfred's side.

David looked around the chapel and was pleased to see it nearly full. His mother and relatives were sitting on the left side. David recognized several London acquaintances and many of the servants from Keynsham Hall on the right side. And then, standing in the doorway, was Lucinda. She looked like an angel surrounded by the soft light of the narrow windows. Dressed in white, the top of her shoulders bared, and white flowers in her short, dark curls. She caught his eye and gave him a smile of the purest light. And then the smallest of winks.

Lucinda was no angel, but he didn't want an angel. He wanted an equal.

Miss Antigone Merritt carefully arranged the long train of her sister's wedding dress. She hugged Persephone and then took her place in front of her, beside Lucinda. Mr. Merritt held out his arm to his elder daughter, and the organist began to play the wedding march. Everyone in the room stood and watched the procession. Miss Merritt looked strikingly radiant in her wedding attire.

The ceremony began. David paid little attention to what the rector said; he was much too focused on Lucinda. And then at last, it was over. He got to escort her out of the chapel, following behind the bride and groom.

"You almost made me laugh at least a half dozen times," Lucinda whispered. "You stared at me the entire ceremony—it was disconcerting."

"You will have to get used to it," he whispered back.

David assisted Lucinda into a carriage, and then Miss

Antigone. He shook hands with several of the guests as he worked his way back to the front of the chapel. The rector was not there. David looked around the vestibule and saw him dressed in his normal clothes, once again carrying his box of robes.

"There you are, Rector. Would you like to stay for the wedding party at Keynsham Hall?" David asked politely. "Or shall I direct the driver to take you home?"

"I am fond of parties," the rector said. "But perhaps I should return home to St. Ivy's. In my hurry, I failed to mention to my wife where I was going."

"Give my apologies to Mrs.—" David began. "I am afraid I do not know your surname, Rector. In all of the rush, I seem to have lost my manners."

The rector merely smiled. "Mr. Topliffe, pleased to meet you properly, Mr. Randall."

"Topliffe?" David echoed as he shook the man's hand.

"That's the name I was born to."

"Topliffe," David repeated. "Topliffe. I have heard that name before. But where?"

"Really?" the rector said. "'Tisn't a common name."

"Bertha Topliffe!" David said more loudly than he meant to.

Mr. Topliffe exhaled slowly. "Were you acquainted with my late sister, Mr. Randall?"

David shook his head. "I am afraid not, Mr. Topliffe. But I did have the pleasure of making Mrs. Burntwood's acquaintance. She said your sister was the author Mrs. Smith."

"Aye," Mr. Topliffe said with a sad smile. "She had a talent with words, she did. Forgive me, but I am surprised Mrs. Burntwood told you about her. My sister obviously wrote under a nom de plume."

"My friend and I have been making inquiries throughout England for information about your sister," David explained.

"Whatever for?" he said in surprise.

"My particular friend is most anxious to know Miss Eurydice Emerson's fate," David said.

Mr. Topliffe looked perplexed at first, then said, "Ah, the main character in *She Knew She Was Right*."

"Precisely."

"I am afraid my sister did not live long enough to finish Miss Emerson's story," Mr. Topliffe said.

"Did she leave any indication or notes in her final papers?" David pressed.

"I am embarrassed to say I have not yet gone through my sister's papers that Mrs. Burntwood sent," Mr. Topliffe explained. "The grief is still too near."

"Of course," David said. "Thank you again for coming so quickly and filling in."

Mr. Topliffe nodded and stepped into the carriage. As he shut the carriage door, he said, "Should your particular friend wish to call upon me, I would be happy to receive them. Perhaps it is time to see my sister's final words. A very good day to you, Mr. Randall."

"And to you, Mr. Topliffe."

Twenty-One

"LADY PERSEPHONE ADLINGTON," LUCINDA SAID, waving her arms grandly in an exaggerated bow.

Persephone gave her a quick embrace. "You are the first to call me by my new title."

"And how does the name sound to you, Lady Persephone?"

"I love it!" Persephone exclaimed.

Lucinda laughed. Antigone unpinned Persephone's veil and unhooked the long lace train from her white wedding gown. Persephone twirled in the mirror, raising her skirt just enough for Lucinda to see her crinoline cage. Lucinda laughed again and thought her friend glowed with happiness. Antigone laughed too.

"I proclaim you ready to dance," Lucinda said.

Persephone linked arms with both Lucinda and Antigone, and they walked to the great medieval hall. The large room with an enormously high ceiling was full of fashionably dressed people. A quartet of string players played a lively country dance. Couples formed in the center of the room to create the set of dancers. Lord Adlington claimed Persephone's hand. Antigone left to speak to her parents, and Lucinda stood alone on the side of the room.

Lucinda looked around to see if she had any acquaintances in the party when she saw Mrs. Randall and Lady Mary Adlington walking arm in arm toward her. Mrs. Randall smiled at Lucinda, but it looked more wistful than happy. The dowager countess only gave her a small nod. Lucinda bowed to the older women.

"How do you do, Miss Leavitt?" Mrs. Randall asked.

"Much better. Thank you, Mrs. Randall," Lucinda said. "Congratulations, Lady Mary, on your son's marriage."

Lady Mary gave her another curt nod and walked away, releasing her hold on Mrs. Randall's arm.

"I suppose I shall have to beg for your arm," Mrs. Randall said. "Shall we take a turn around the room?"

Lucinda allowed Mrs. Randall to place her hand inside Lucinda's elbow and led her to the edge of the great hall. Lucinda did not know what to say or what not to say. She did not know to what level David's mother was in his confidence. Mrs. Randall did not speak either, but nodded genially to her acquaintances and continued her circle of the room.

They had nearly completed an entire turn when at last Mrs. Randall said, "You remind me of your mother. She was also very beautiful. Irish, but beautiful."

"I did not know you were at all acquainted with my mother."

"I am afraid I only met her once," Mrs. Randall said. "I was not as attentive as I ought to have been."

Lucinda said nothing.

"Nor have I given you the attention you deserve, Miss Leavitt," Mrs. Randall said. "I cannot go back and behave better, but I do hope you will allow me, in future, to be your friend."

Lucinda gulped. Mrs. Randall had snubbed her mother for her nationality and her working-class background. And instead of telling a motherless Lucinda about her menses and burgeoning womanhood, she had told her father to send her to finishing school. And after Lucinda returned from school, Mrs. Randall hadn't ever called. She'd only left her card.

Yet here Mrs. Randall was, offering her friendship. Part of Lucinda wished to scorn it. For her mother's sake. For her own. But Mrs. Randall was David's mother, and she knew all about Lucinda's humble origins. And yet she was clearly trying to extend the olive branch.

"Please, call me Lucinda," she said at last. "My friends call me Lucinda."

"Lucinda is a very pretty name," Mrs. Randall said.

"It means light," Lucinda said, not knowing what else to say.

"How appropriate," Mrs. Randall said.

"What is?"

Lucinda looked up to see David standing in front of them with his cockiest of smiles. Lucinda could not help but grin.

"Lucinda was telling me her name means light," Mrs. Randall said.

"Very appropriate," David agreed. "Mother, do you mind if I steal Miss Leavitt for the waltz?"

"Not at all."

Mrs. Randall released her hold on Lucinda's arm, and Lucinda placed her hand into David's outstretched one. He brought his other hand to her waist and pulled her closer to him as they danced.

"Where have you been?" Lucinda asked.

"Were you looking for me?"

"No, no," Lucinda said quickly, shaking her head.

"Are you sure?" David asked.

"I might have noticed you were not present," Lucinda allowed.

"Do you wish to know where I was?"

Lucinda shrugged nonchalantly, and she heard David laugh. She looked up into his smiling face, and her heart began to beat faster. He leaned his head closer to hers and whispered, "I've found her at last."

"*Who?*"

"Eurydice Emerson."

Lucinda and David sat on one side of the carriage and her father sat on the other.

"Now, where are we going again, Lucinda?" her father asked.

"To meet Mr. Topliffe, the rector of St. Ivy's parish," Lucinda explained. "He is the brother of a recently deceased author who died before completing her story. He is in possession of her final papers, and I am hoping to find some clue to how she would have ended it."

"All this effort is for a story?"

"It is not about the story," David said before Lucinda could. "It's about unfinished business."

When they arrived at the small rectory next to St. Ivy's Church, David alighted from the carriage, helped Lucinda out, and held the door for her father. They had not yet reached the front step of the rectory when Mr. Topliffe opened the door to his house and invited them in. He led them to a comfortable sitting room with chairs that had seen many years of service. His wife served them tea, and he took out a small box, opening the lid.

"This is everything Mrs. Burntwood sent," he said solemnly.

Lucinda touched the top paper, but was unable to pick it up. Her hands could not perform such small tasks yet. David did not wait to be asked, but was instantly at her side. He picked up the paper and turned it over. The first dozen or so pages were letters from Mr. Topliffe to his sister. David continued to turn the papers over. There were several letters from the editor, Mr. Gibbs. David was nearly to the bottom of the pile, and Lucinda began to despair.

He picked up the second-to-last paper and turned it over, revealing the last page. This paper was written by a different hand. It was a neat scrawl, but very tiny. Lucinda had to peer closer to read the words.

> *It pained her, but Eurydice Emerson knew she was right. She could not marry where she did not love.*
>
> *"Mr. Thisbe, I am honored by your offer of marriage," she said. "I think you are a most estimable man. But it is impossible for me to accept it. I can only wish you happiness and God's greatest blessings in your future life."*
>
> *"I hope you are not deluded by your other suitor," he said. "Lord Dunstan's life has not been what your future husband's should have been."*
>
> *Eurydice flushed with anger.*
>
> *"Please, sir. Let us speak of this no more. It will not be pleasing to either party."*
>
> *"Very well, Miss Emerson. I bid you adieu."*
>
> *Eurydice could not speak. She turned from her spurned suitor and fled farther into the garden. Her tears fell like rain from her eyes. She stumbled to her knees and rested her head on a stone bench. What great crime had Lord Dunstan committed to cause Mr. Thisbe to feel such scorn?*
>
> *"Miss Emerson."*

Behind her stood none other than Lord Dunstan. He looked handsomer than ever. He stepped toward her.

"My dear girl, what is amiss?"

Eurydice dabbed her handkerchief at her eyes and managed to get to her feet. She could not quite look Lord Dunstan in the eye.

"Mr. Thisbe said the most unpleasant things about you, sir."

"What did he say?"

Eurydice could only shake her head.

"I should have told you before, Miss Emerson—Eurydice," Lord Dunstan said. "In my youth, I committed many follies. The most grievous one is that I was a free trader for several years. You would call it smuggling. Indeed, that is how I earned my fortune and saved the family estate. I promise I am no longer engaged in the illegal trade and that in future, I will be upright before the law and the Lord."

Lord Dunstan placed his hand on her shoulder, and Eurydice turned back to look at him.

"My lord, I cannot say that I approve of such behavior," she began, "but I believe a person can change, and I believe you when you say that you have changed."

Lord Dunstan took each of Eurydice's hands and kissed them. "My dearest Eurydice, say you will be my wife."

"I cannot," she said. "I am sorry. Although I hold a great regard for you, I do not love you."

"Perhaps, with time, you could learn to love me?" he suggested.

"Love is not a subject that can be taught," Eurydice said, and gently pulled her hands from his. "Love can only be felt by your heart and echoed in the darkest corners of your soul."

Lord Dunstan nodded, stepping back from her.

"I appreciate your honesty, Miss Emerson," he said with a bow. "Should you ever need my assistance, please know that I would gladly offer it to you."

"Thank you," she said. "Goodbye, dear friend."

Eurydice left the garden and returned to the house. But her home no longer fit her—it was like a favorite dress she'd outgrown.

She went into her childhood bedchamber and began placing her clothes in a trunk. There was a great wide world out there, and it was time for her to go and discover it. Eurydice . . .

Clearly Bertha Topliffe had intended to write more. But she never did. She left her greatest work unfinished. Lucinda looked up and saw the eyes of three men upon her, waiting expectedly.

"Eurydice Emerson knew she was right."

"And?" her father asked.

"And?" Mr. Topliffe questioned.

"And?" David prompted.

"She refused them both and decided to leave home for the wider world."

"I knew it!" David said and punched the air. "I told you that from the start. She wasn't in love with either of them."

"David Randall knew *he* was right," Lucinda quipped.

And they all laughed.

Epilogue

A YEAR LATER, LUCINDA BREATHED in the smell of freshly cut lumber and recently painted orange trim. The newly rebuilt countinghouse on Tooley Street now boasted three private offices: Mr. Leavitt, Owner; Mr. David Randall, Owner; and Miss Lucinda Leavitt, Chief Financial Officer. Lucinda's office had three windows that were covered in morning frost. She walked to the windows and looked out at the new buildings among the remnants of the destructive fire that had nearly cost her life. The River Thames flowed past with a steadiness that reassured her.

She sat at her desk and looked at her mother's portrait hanging prominently on the wall of her office. Lucinda felt warm and loved every time she looked at her mother's brown eyes and beautiful face. Her mother had understood how it felt to be a part of two societies without belonging to either of them. Lucinda was not sure where she fit in society anymore, but it no longer mattered to her. She had a friend who cared for her. A father who adored her. And a fiancé who loved her.

Lucinda no longer felt unfinished.

She felt complete.

Whole.

Lucinda took off her gloves. She wiggled her stiff, scarred fingers to loosen them. She carefully turned the cover of the first ledger and picked up her pen. Her hand clenched, but she held the pen determinedly. She was strong. She could hold this pen in her hand. She could accomplish any task.

Lucinda completed the first page.

The second.

The third.

She dipped her pen into the ink and painstakingly turned the ledger to the fourth page when she heard a knock at the door. She set the pen down on the desk.

"Come in."

David opened the door and closed it behind him. He gave her his familiar cocky grin and lifted his eyebrows.

"Yes, David?"

"Do you like your new office?"

"I adore my new office," she said, crossing the room to the man she loved. "And do you like yours?"

David took her hands in his and kissed each one. "Yes, but what I like best is that it is right next to yours."

"Very conveniently placed," Lucinda said, trying hard not to giggle.

"Very," David agreed.

Lucinda wrapped her arms around his neck and kissed him long and lingeringly on the lips. And just like Miss Eurydice Emerson, Lucinda knew she was right where she wanted to be.

Author's Note

WHEN I READ ELIZABETH GASKELL'S *Wives and Daughters* for the first time, I did not know Mrs. Gaskell had died before completing the novel. I eagerly turned the massive Victorian tome's pages and was concerned as I got closer to the end that there was too much to wrap up and not enough pages to do it. Then I turned the last page, and I saw the editor's concluding remarks stating Mrs. Gaskell had died and these were her intentions for the conclusion. I felt cheated. Upset. And I wondered what it would have been like to be reading it serially.

Wives and Daughters was published in chapters, or serially, in *Cornhill Magazine* from August 1864 to January 1866. Part of the first paragraph of the fictional editor's remarks in *She Knew She Was Right* is taken from the real editor's note about Mrs. Gaskell in *Wives and Daughters*. Unlike the editor in my story, Gaskell's editor assures the reader the two main characters did indeed marry and live happily ever after.

Many Victorian authors' novels were published serially, including Charles Dickens, who died leaving *The Mystery of Edwin Drood* unfinished. But it's his book, *A Tale of Two Cities*, that became the inspiration for Mrs. Smith's first novel, *A Tale of Two Towns*. Anthony Trollope was another prolific Victorian writer, and I used the title of his novel *He Knew He Was Right* to create Mrs. Smith's *She Knew She Was Right*. My favorite novel by the author Elizabeth Gaskell is *North and South*, and so I gave a nod to it with the title of Mrs. Smith's fictional novel, *East and West*.

King Henry I announced the building of Reading Abbey in 1121. In 1855, the Reading Corporation purchased the land for the Forbury Gardens. Jane Austen and her sister Cassandra attended school in the Abbey Gateway in 1785. In 1861, the Abbey Gateway collapsed in a gale and Sir George Gilbert Scott, a Victorian architect known for his Gothic Revival work, was hired to restore it.

On June 22, 1861, a fire broke out in Scovell's warehouse. This event is known as the Tooley Street Fire of 1861. More than eleven acres in London were burned, and some parts of the fire took nearly three weeks to be put out completely. The River Thames was truly on fire because of all the oil and tallow that poured into the river from the warehouses, which were also on fire. Fireman Tozer and Superintendent James Braidwood were real people. Braidwood died in the explosion described in the story, and he was accorded a hero's funeral.

The steel framework of the crinoline cage (picture a large birdcage from your waist to your ankle) made it impossible to wrap a rug around a woman's dress to extinguish the flames. The oxygen from underneath the skirt kept the fire burning. Clothing was very flammable, and people of all ages died by being burned to death, including the wife of American author Henry David Longfellow in 1861. Fanny Appleton Longfellow accidently started her clothing on fire with melted sealing wax. Longfellow burned his hands and face trying to save his wife, but she died the next morning from her injuries.

Amelia Jenks Bloomer was a women's rights activist. She founded a feminist magazine in 1849 called *The Lily*, where she advocated women's dress reform among other women's rights issues, including suffrage, better education, wider employment, and fair pay. She thought that women's clothing was impractical and uncomfortable. Inspired by a colleague's traveling costume (Elizabeth Smith Miller), Amelia Jenks Bloomer made her own pantaloons with a shortened skirt and promoted them in her magazine. Thousands of women wrote to the magazine asking for patterns and instructions on how to make the pantaloons. Dress reform outraged conservatives, and they nicknamed her pantaloons "bloomers." Although not widely accepted, Victorian dress reform was an important step for feminism.

Acknowledgments

DEAR READER, THANK YOU FOR picking up my book and taking the time to read *my* last words. The writing and publishing process is a long and hard one, and there are so many people I need to thank for helping me along the way.

I would like to give an impossibly big thank-you to the Swoon Reads team: Jean Feiwel, Lauren Scobell, Holly West, and Kat Brzozowski. To my editor, Emily Settle, I am so grateful for your amazing insight into my characters and your great eye for detail. My book is better because of you. Thank you, Katie Klimowicz, for the unforgettable cover you created. I really appreciate all the incredible work from my copyeditor, Kayley Hoffman, my production editor, Ilana Worrell, and my publicist, Madison Furr. There are not enough words, even last ones, to tell you what your work has meant to me.

Cheers to the Novel Nineteens debut group for swapping stories and wisdom. And a special shout-out to my Swoon Sisters (other Swoon Reads authors). I'm so grateful to have your support and sassiness on my publishing journey. You are all so talented and I'm humbled to be among you.

I would tip my hat (if I wore one) to my amazing beta readers: Maren, Katie, Dannielle, Erin, Angie, Mylee, and Eva.

I am so blessed to have a supportive family. To my sisters, Michelle and Stacy, I don't know what I would do without you. You have always been my best friends and my greatest fans. Thank you for loving me and everything that I write. To my brothers, Keith and Steve, thank you for teaching me that humor is possible (and essential) in every situation. To my mom and dad, thank you for believing that I could do anything and supporting me when I tried. To my kids, I am so grateful that I get to call you mine. You challenge me and surprise me daily. Being your mom is my greatest adventure so far.

And finally to my husband, Jon, who believed in my dreams even when I doubted them. Thank you for encouraging me to keep writing when I got discouraged. You are the Darcy to my Elizabeth, the Rochester to my Jane, the Howl to my Sophie. I love you so much, and I am so lucky to have a happily ever after with you.

DID YOU KNOW...

readers like you helped to get this book published?

Join our book-obsessed community and help us discover awesome new writing talent.

1 

Write it.

Share your original YA manuscript.

2 

Read it.

Discover bright new bookish talent.

3 

Share it.

Discuss, rate, and share your faves.

4 

Love it.

Help us publish the books you love.

Share your own manuscript or dive between the pages at **swoonreads.com** or by downloading the **Swoon Reads app**.

Check out more books chosen for publication by readers like you.

READER
Swoon
READS
APPROVED

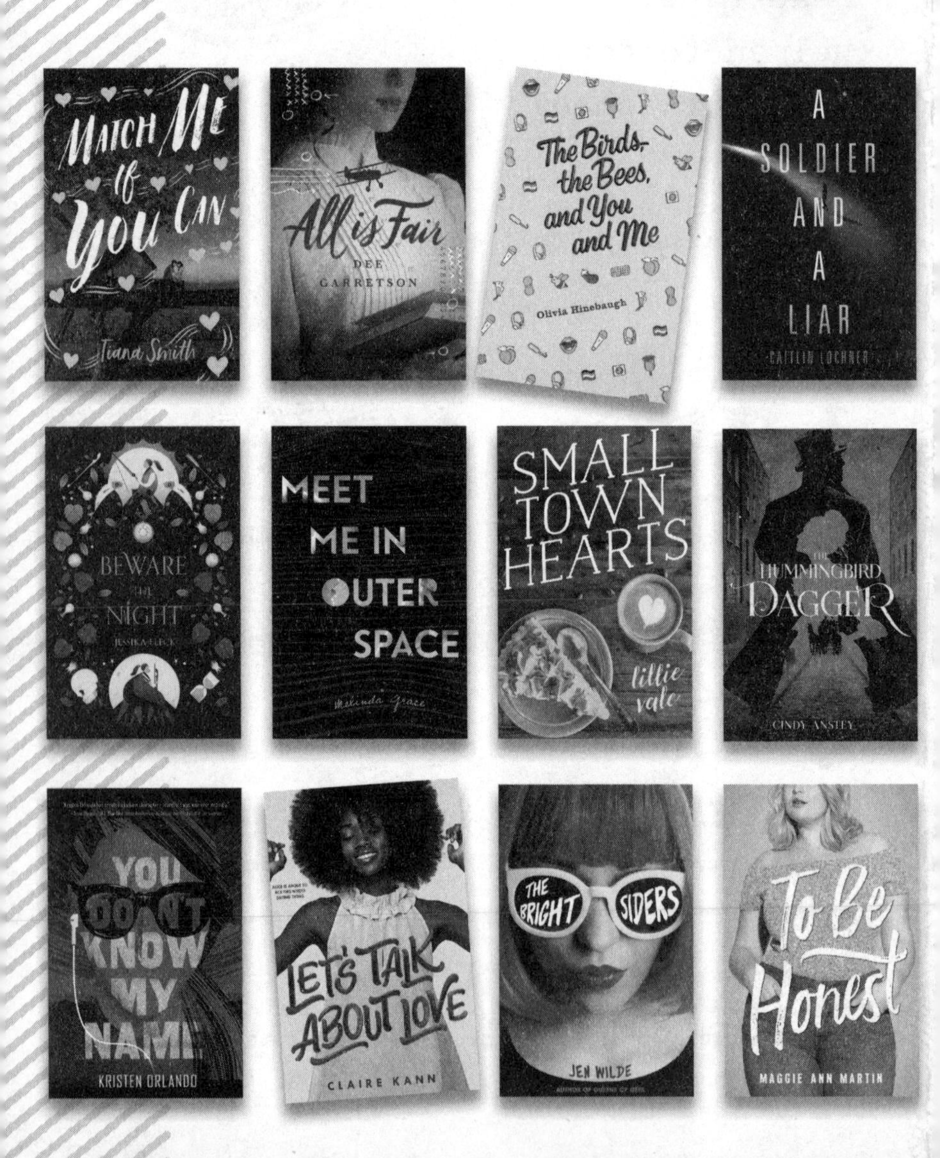